Saving Her

MANCINI LEGACY SERIES
BOOK 2

NATALIE ARTHUR

The Mancini Legacy Series books are all stand alone with NO cheating and HEA.

Even though they are standalone, they are best enjoyed if read in order. There is also mention of characters from my Cimaruta MC Chicago series.

❀ Created with Vellum

Acknowledgments

Jeff, thank you for answering all my questions no matter what time or how many I had. I'm so grateful that I have you and Stacey in my life.

Jessica, you are summer and I am winter. Always.

Danni, this journey is so crazy! Thank you for being here with me!

JD, thank you for spending late nights with and making sure I listened even when I didn't want to. Love you.

Nicole, I'm forever grateful that you're in my life.

Carissa, thank you for everything you do.

Arthur, you've always supported me no matter how crazy my ideas are. I love you so much.

Mom, you've always been my biggest supporter and I don't know where I'd be without you.

Caoimhe-Lea, you drive me absolutely fucking crazy. But I wouldn't have it any other way. Love you.

Taye, and everyone I'm forgetting who has supported my crazy ideas and continue to be with me, thank you. I truly couldn't do this without all of you.

Information

No part of this book or graphics were made with AI.
HUMAN CREATION ONLY

Saving Her has NO cheating with a guaranteed HEA.
It is second book in my Mancini Legacy Series and is
connected to my Cimaruta MC Chicago Series.

There are not a lot of dark moments or dark issues in
my books, there still are the occasions that have to do
with kidnapping, domestic abuse, and assault.

Check out my website for current news and trigger
warnings.
Mancini Legacy and Cimaruta MC Chicago family
trees.
Nataliearthurbooks.com

Mancini Legacy and Cimaruta MC Dictionary

Cage - Motorized vehicle with four wheels. (Cars)

Chicago Panthers - Professional baseball team.

Chicago Redhawks - Professional hockey team.

Cimaruta MC, Chicago - Chicago Motorcycle club, Mother charter

Cut - Vest that patched in members of the MC wear to identify who they are and their rank.

Lake Renegade Township - Town owned by the Mancini family.

Lucciola Island - 'Firefly' Island, owned by the Mancini family and located in Massachusetts.

Lucciola Memorial Hospital - Hospital in Lake Renegade Township.

Mancini Grill - 5-star restaurant located inside the Legacy Hotel.

Rockers - Top rocker has the club's name on it, the bottom rocker has the club's location.

Sprite Lake Village - Town in Illinois, owned by the Laurent family.

The Legacy Hotel - Hotel in downtown Chicago owned by the Mancini family.

Galway - Town in Ireland.

ITALIAN

Amore - Love.

Coglione - Asshole.

Colomba mia - My dove.

Cugino - Cousin.

Cuore mio - My heart.

Dolcezza - Sweetness.

Famiglia - Family.

Figlio - Son.

Fratello - Brother.

Il mio mondo - My world.

Il mio pinguino - My penguin.

Mai Andato - Never Gone.

Mi dispiace - I'm sorry.

Mi passerotta - My little sparrow.

Nonno - Grandfather.

Nonna - Grandmother.

Ti abbiamo aspettato - We waited for you.

Ti voglio bene - I love you.

Zio - Uncle.

Zia -Aunt.

IRISH

Aintín - Aunty

Is í Gàidhlig ár gcéad teanga - Gaelic is our first language.

M'anam - My soul

Mo stór - My treasure.

FRENCH

D'accord petite sœur - Okay little sister

Je t'aime et Lorenzo - I love you and Lorenzo

Je t'aime - I love you

Je vous aime tous les deux - I love you both

Princesse - Princess

Toujours - Always

Toujours mes frères - Always my brothers

Tu es ma princesse - You are my princess

MANCINI FAMILY

Pietro & Alessia
Grandparents

Enea (T)
Son

Antonio (T)
Son

Leonardo (T)
Son

Gráinne
Daughter-in-law

Rosaura
Daughter-in-law

Sebastiano*
Grandson

Salvatore^
Grandson

Domenico*
Grandson

Fiorella^
Granddaughter

Lorenzo+
Grandson

Gianluca^
Grandson

Giovanna+
Granddaughter

Rowan
Great Grandson

(T) = Triplets
* = Twins
+ = Twins
^ = Triplets

MANCINI FAMILY

Antonio (T)

Enea (T)

Gráinne

Leonardo (T)

Rosaura

Sebastiano*

Salvatore^

Schuyler

Sansone

Fiorella^

Domenico*

Lorenzo+

Gianluca^

Giovanna+

Declan

Rowan

(T) = Triplets
* = Twins
+ = Twins
^ = Triplets

FAUSTO & LUNA
GRANDPARENTS
GIACOMO
SON
CAITRÍONA
DAUGHTER IN LAW
CELESTINO
GRANDSON
FRANCESCO
GRANDSON
SAOIRSE
GREAT GRANDDAUGHTER
ISABELLA
GRANDDAUGHTER
LUCIANA
GRANDDAUGHTER
GRAYSON
GREAT GRANDSON
BASTIANINI
FAMILY

GIACOMO
CAITRÍONA
CELESTINO
ISABELLA
FRANCESCO
LUCIANA
MAEVE
RÓNÁN
SAOIRSE
GRAYSON
BASTIANINI
FAMILY

Ardghal +
Niamh

O'CALLAGHAN

Keegan
Aodhán
Fintan
Rónán
Luciana
Grayson

Cimaruta MC

President - Giacomo 'Forza' Bastianini

Vice President - Celestino 'Giustizia' Bastianini

Sgt-At-Arms - Francesco 'Bestia' Bastianini

Treasurer - Luciana 'Fuoco' Bastianini

Secretary - Isabella 'Dolce' Bastianini

Historian - Caitríona 'Forte' Bastianini

Road Captain - Connor 'Azrael' Byrne

Chaplain - Brennan 'Raziel' Doyle

Enforcer - Liam 'Amante' Murphy

Enforcer - Valentino 'Ombra' Marconi

Enforcer - Romana 'Fantasma' Vietti

Enforcer - Mitchell 'Granchio' Harris

Enforcer - Hollis 'Cavallo' Taylor

Enforcer - Rónán 'Ghiaccio' O'Callaghan

Enforcer - Fintan 'Toro' O'Callaghan

Prospect - Anthony Grimes

Laurent Family

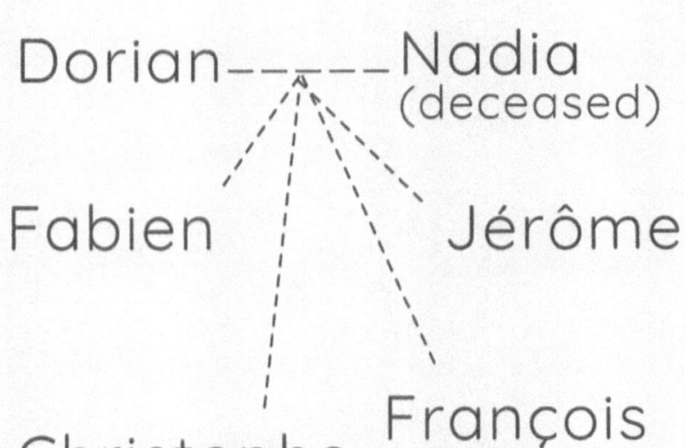

Contents

Saving Her

Chapter One

Sebastiano

Being the oldest child is never easy. When you're the oldest, you're responsible for the younger ones. So, since I'm one whole minute older than my identical twin brother, Domenico—a fact you can bet your ass I remind him of often—that responsibility falls to me. We also have twin siblings, Lorenzo and Giovanna, that are one year younger than us. I don't know what my parents were thinking, having us so close together... wait, never mind. I don't want to know.

Long before we were born, there was a war between our family and the Laurent family. It started back in Europe before my grandparents came here to America. There were times when the war would intensify. When Dom and I were three, it escalated further than it ever had before. Lorenzo and Giovanna were kidnapped and my parents were told that they had been killed. My papà had explained that without solid proof that it was the Laurents, there was no way to go after them.

I've spent my whole life wondering what it would've been like to have them grow up with us. A life where my mam didn't cry every day for years over the loss of her babies.

Twenty-three years later, we found them. Or should I say Dom's stomach lead us to them. Domenico and I were at a mall in Cambridge, Massachusetts when we saw Lorenzo and Giovanna. They had lived their entire lives about three hours away from us in Springfield, yet somehow, we never crossed paths. It took Dom being hungry and us stopping at the mall in another state to find them.

Finding them has made some of the emptiness and anger that I've carried around all my life go away. We also got some closure and answers as to why they were taken and who took them.

It was Dorian Laurent. He stole them and raised them as his own. At the time, Dorian was second-incommand of the Springfield Mafia, under his father Renaud.

At first he tried to say that he found the twins crying and alone, which we all knew was a lie. Later, he admitted the reason he kidnapped them was to show his father that he was ready to take over.

Even though they live with us now, Enzo and Gia still talk to the Laurent boys, their 'brothers' that they grew up with. I'm trying to understand and be nice about it, but it's so fucking unfair. Every time I see them, or hear my brother or sister talking to them, it makes me so angry. Even though logically, I know it wasn't the boys' fault, they had the life with the twins that we should've.

In this past year since finding them, Giovanna has gotten married to a teammate of Dom's, Declan O'Reilly, and they have the most adorable son named Rowan. He's now six months old and I make all kinds of excuses to go next door to play with him. I love watching my sister being a mam. After spending most of my life without her, I want to spend all the time I can with her and Rowan. And Declan, I guess.

Lorenzo applied to Wildcat Law so that he could stay close to us. Of course, he got accepted and has started his first year. He's the best little brother and I love having him here, especially since Dom travels a lot for hockey. The three of us share a house in Evanston. It's an easy commute for Enzo to get to school, for Dom to get to the United Center, and for me to get to work.

Declan, Dom, and Fiorella's boyfriend, Cillian

McGregor, play for the Chicago Redhawks. Dom's their starting goalie, Declan's their star defenseman and assistant captain. Cillian's their number one right wing player and captain of the team.

Gia and I go to all their home games together, along with our triplet cousins, Salvatore, Fiorella and Gianluca.

I work for our family business, Mancini Legacy Enterprises. We own several businesses, restaurants, and even a hotel here in Chicago.

I'm the head of our IT Department. My job is to make sure all our software and security is up to date. I'm also in charge of maintaining all the websites and apps for every business we own. Out of the seven Mancinis in my generation, I'm the only one who works for our family business. After Lorenzo finishes law school and takes the bar, he'll join us to be our in-house counsel. Giovanna was going to school to be a doctor, but she's postponed that for now. She says maybe she'll continue when Rowan is older. That little man has her wrapped around his chubby little finger.

Schuyler

I wake up and stretch, clenching my jaw to keep from crying out from the pain that's radiating through my body. Turning to look at the other side of the bed, I feel a sense of relief when I see it's empty. I run my hand over the area and find that it's cold. I puff out the breath I didn't even realize I'd been holding in. That's when I see the bathroom door is closed and hear the shower running. That sick feeling settles in my stomach again.

I hear the shower turn off and see Blaine come strutting out of the bathroom. Before all this started, I loved looking at him. To me he's always looked like Zac Efron, those blue eyes, that toned body...down to that boyish smile that used to melt my heart. Now it makes me want to vomit.

"Morning, baby. Did you want breakfast?"

I stare at him, then shake my head no.

He's talking to me as if it's just another fucking day. Like he didn't attack me last night.

We've been together for three years. Six months ago I tried to leave him. When I wouldn't come back, he threatened to take my baby sister Mirabelle and make her his. I couldn't take that chance. So here I am, back with him again.

Last night when we went out to dinner, we ran into my friend Salvatore Mancini. He's an officer with the Chicago Police Department. Blaine knows Sal and yet last night after drinking too much, we got home and he accused me of sleeping with Sal. Like an idiot, I tried to reason with him. I know I should've let it go, but I fought back. Now looking at myself in the bathroom mirror, I wish I'd just let it go. There are marks on my stomach, chest, and a handprint on my neck. He never leaves marks on my face.

I get in the shower and carefully wash my body. I need to figure out how to leave him and still keep Mira safe. Blaine works for the biggest company here in Chicago and that company is owned by the Mancini family. Rumor is they're mafia. The Mancinis own a lot of businesses here, and from what Blaine has told me, his dad is good friends with Leonardo Mancini. I know his dad abuses his mom because I've seen the marks on her. She's also the most timid woman I've ever met. I don't want to end up like her.

I pull out my special concealer and cover up all the marks and bruises that are forming. When I'm satisfied that I've gotten all of them, I get dressed for work. I'm a Lieutenant Paramedic for the Evanston Fire Department and I'm stationed at Firehouse 5. Our shifts are twenty-four hours long, then we have forty-eight hours off. I used to love my days off but since this new situation started with Blaine? I dread them. Luckily, he doesn't live with me. He stays over when he feels like it, which lately has been all the time. I love when he goes on business trips and these past few months, he's had a lot of business trips. Sometimes he's away for an entire week and I wonder if he's met someone. I hope he has, because that would solve all of my problems. I head downstairs to get my things so I can leave. When I reach for my bag, he startles me by grabbing my arm.

"Were you going to leave without saying goodbye?" He frowns and backs me up against the wall.

"No. I was going to say bye after I got my things

together. And I still need to take my vitamins," I say as I stare into his eyes. "I have to get moving or I'll be late."

He kisses me while I try not to gag.

"I love you." He kisses his way down my neck and chest, then leaves a mark on my chest, smiling at what he did.

I try to leave without him realizing I haven't said it back.

"Aren't you forgetting something?"

I give him a blank look. "I don't think so," I say, pretending to look around.

He gets an ugly look on his face and I do my best not to flinch when he slams his hand on the wall near my head.

"You didn't say you love me." He clenches his jaw.

"Sorry, I thought I did. I love you. I have to go..."

He steps back slowly, still glaring at me.

"I'll see you tomorrow after work."

I nod at him and duck under his arm to head to the kitchen to take my vitamins.

I get in my car and head to the station, stopping at the beach along the way to add more concealer to the new mark he left on me. Sitting there, I slam my hand on the steering wheel and take several deep breaths. I hate him so fucking much.

I head to Star-Coffee to get coffee for the guys at the station. I make sure they make Cap's extra special. My captain is Michael Jeffries and from the day I started at Station 5, he's always looked out for me. It's nice, because I never really had a dad. He'll give me shit if I don't pull my share around the firehouse, but at the end of the day he makes sure I'm okay. He even invites Mira and me over for barbecues with his family. And his wife Lynn? She's taken Mira and me under her 'love umbrella'—her words, not mine.

Mira and I grew up in foster care. I remember our birth parents but she doesn't. I was seven when our father shot our mother, then turned the gun on himself. They said he'd been so drugged up he probably didn't even know what he was doing. It happened while I was at school. When I got off the bus at home, all I saw were police cars and ambulances everywhere. Besides that there's not a lot that I remember about that day. Except that somehow I found Mira and I wouldn't let her go. The police think that because our father had been so high, he forgot Mira was in the apartment with them, which saved her life. Because if he had remembered, he probably would've killed her too.

We were lucky because the social worker that we were assigned to made sure we stayed together the whole time we were in foster care. When I turned eighteen, I filed to be Mira's guardian. She was thirteen at the time. Our social worker helped me apply to the Chicago Fire Department. While I waited for my acceptance, I worked other jobs to support Mira and myself. She's now eighteen and will be starting at Blue University here in Chicago. I'm glad she stayed close for school. This past weekend, Cap and Lynn helped me move her into the dorms. I'm extremely thankful that Mira is out of the house now because when Blaine gets into one of his moods, I don't have to hide it from her anymore.

Tomorrow night's the annual Police and Firefighters Ball. Unfortunately, I have to take Blaine with me. Blaine wasn't always this abusive. The first two years we were together, we had a lot of fun. The abusive part started about a year ago. He started getting jealous and then one night he got drunk and hit me. Of course he swore up and down that he would never do it again. But we all know how that turned out. Who knows what this year will be like. I wish I could be on shift tomorrow night.

There's one good thing, though. Blaine is usually well-behaved in public. He doesn't show the ugly side of himself to other people. And because we'll be surrounded by firefighters and police officers, he probably won't cause trouble.

My station is a single-engine station, which means we only have one engine in our house, Engine 25. Because of this, there are only three people working per shift. Our shift is usually Cap, me, and Rhys. I'm the driver and Rhys is our backstep. But since Rhys is on vacation, we have what we call a floater.

I stop to give the him one of the coffees before I head to Cap's office.

"Hi. I'm Schuyler," I say while I hand him his coffee.

"Thanks. I'm Anthony."

"Nice to meet you." I smile, heading over to knock on Cap's door.

I hear him yell, "What?"

I laugh and open the door. "Morning coffee, your grumpiness."

He snorts as I hand him his coffee.

"You're late." He looks at his watch.

"Psh. I'm not late. I was giving the floater his coffee." I laugh at the look on his face.

"Wait...You served the floater before me?" He raises an eyebrow at me while I nod, giving him an innocent smile.

"Yep. How's Mama?" Lynn insists Mira and I call her Mama.

"She's good. You and Mira need to come over for dinner soon. She misses you."

"She's coming to the ball, right?"

"Of course she is. She got a new dress for it, even. You bringing Dickweed?"

I snort and choke on my drink. Cap hates Blaine and he doesn't understand why I went back to him. He also refuses to call him by his name. He makes up new names to call him all the time.

He laughs and tosses me a napkin.

"Yes, Blaine's coming." I make faces at him as I wipe the coffee that's dribbled down my chin.

"You know you need to leave his ass. He ain't good enough for you."

He's staring at me and studying my expression. Fuck. I need to leave before he realizes I'm lying. He knows me too well.

"I have to change. Is the floater making breakfast?"

"Yeah, I told him to start when you got here. And stop changing the subject." He's still staring at me. It's like he can see the bruises under my shirt and on my neck.

I walk really fast to my locker to grab my clothes and head to the bathroom to change, making sure all of my marks are still covered up. I hope we don't have any tough calls today.

Sebastiano

I pull out my phone when I hear it ring and look at it. My cousin Salvatore's face appears. I sit on one of the lounge chairs by the pool and answer his call.

"Hey, Sal."

"Hey! Are you busy tomorrow night?"

"Why? You bored? Need a wingman for something?"

"Well, kind of. It's the Police and Firefighters Ball tomorrow night and I completely forgot about it. I don't want to ask someone because it's such short notice. Want to come with me?"

"As long as I don't have to wear a dress, I'm in."

I hear him laughing.

"No dress, but you need a tux."

"Shit. Seriously? Maybe you should take Enzo or Dom. Or hell, take Luca. I mean, he IS your brother."

"Well, I thought I'd take all of you. I can get tickets for everyone."

"Ugh. Fine. Let's get a group chat going and see if they wanna to go."

I can hear him laughing and I hang up on him.

I start a group chat with Sal, Dom, Enzo, Gia, Declan, Rella, Cillian and Luca.

Sebastiano: Hello?

Domenico: WTF? Don't we already have a group chat?

Lorenzo: Are we planning a bank heist? Is that why we need a new chat?

Giovanna: Seriously, Enzo? That's the first thing you think of? What kind of lawyer are you? Fucking criminal (tongue emoji)

Lorenzo: (angel emoji)

Fiorella: Dork

Sebastiano: SIGH. (eyeball emoji) This chat is for Sal

Salvatore: Maybe this was a bad idea

Giovanna: Well, we wouldn't know because nobody knows why we're in this chat (thinking emoji)

Sebastiano: Just ask, Sal

Fiorella: Yeah, Sal. Ask us

Gianluca: Ask us what?

Domenico: I still don't get why we have two chats going. Why not use the group chat we always use?

Salvatore: OMG. Okay, fine. The Police/Firefighters ball is tomorrow night. Do you all want to go?

Domenico: …

Fiorella: Do I get to dress up?

Giovanna: Do I have to wear a dress?

Gianluca: Will there be single women?

Salvatore: …

Salvatore: I take it back. None of you
are invited

Declan: *snicker*

Lorenzo: Hehe

Cillian: Hey! I want to go! What do we
have to wear?

Domenico: Kiss-ass

Salvatore: (annoyed emoji) Fine, who
wants to go? And yes, you have to
wear a dress and the guys have to
wear a tux

Sebastiano: I'm in

Gianluca: I'm in too

Declan: Gia and I are in

Giovanna: Hey! I don't remember
saying I was in

Fiorella: I'm in and yes, Gia's in

Giovanna: WTF (annoyed emoji)

Lorenzo: Yep, I'm in

Cillian: Yeah of course I'm in

Domenico: We can all get ready here.
Are we going to carpool? Or separate
cars?

Salvatore: Probably easier to carpool.
We should leave by five

Everyone says okay and I go back to laying in the sun. Chicago summers are pleasant, especially when you have a pool to cool off in. I see my cousin Rella coming out back to join me.

"Are you and Gia going shopping for dresses?" It's not like my cousin needs any new dresses. She has an entire closet full of them. I know this because Sal and Luca tease her about her wardrobe all the time.

"No, Gia won't go shopping." She pouts. "She said she's going to wear the one she wore at the auction. Who wears a dress more than once?" She stops and makes a face. "Ugh. I just sounded like an entitled asshole, didn't I?"

I laugh at Rella. "It's ok, cuz. I love you just the way you are. Entitled asshole and all. Where's Cillian?"

She punches me in the arm. "He's at practice. He went with Dom and Declan, they should be home soon." She lays back and suns herself. "Gia said she'll be over with Rowan in a few minutes."

I smile more knowing I'll get to play with Rowan. We just recently started taking him into the pool. He has these really cute floaties he wears on his arms that look like wings. And a floatie that he sits in. It's a dinosaur. Rawr.

Chapter Two

Schuyler

I'm really happy that this shift has been relatively quiet. I didn't have to hide how sore I was, and the pain has only gotten worse as the night went on. We're about thirty minutes from going home and we're all sitting around, relaxing. No one says anything because that could jinx it all and keep us there for who knows how long.

"What time are you and the dummy going to be at the ball?" Cap asks.

"Probably about six? Maybe six-thirty."

Cap nods and gets up to put his dishes away. We see the guys on the next shift walking into the firehouse.

We grab our bags and head out together. I give Cap a hug before getting into my car.

"See you tonight," he says.

I'm excited to see everyone tonight, but of course there's a part of me that's dreading it too. I know Blaine will behave while we're there. But after? It's a crapshoot. I really hope that he decides to just go home after.

Lately, on top of the physical abuse, he's started to try to belittle me with words. It takes a lot out of me to listen to him. I know he's not right...Sometimes he beats me down so much I feel like it would be better if I gave up. I keep reminding myself that I'm doing this for Mira. I can't let him get his hands on her. Ever.

Sebastiano

The house is so loud with everyone here. We're all getting ready for the ball. I turn to watch Gia and Declan. Somewhere in the course of them falling in love, I realized I wanted that too. I want someone to come home to and cuddle with every night, to tell my secrets to. Someone to plan my future with, have a family with, someone to protect. So far I haven't found that someone. The occasional random hookup doesn't give me what I need anymore. I want the one.

Gia comes up and hugs me.

"You look sad, Bastian. Are you okay?" she asks.

She's looking up at me with those big bright green eyes. I can't help but smile at my baby sister.

"I'm ok, Gia," I say softly as I hug her back. "I was just thinking. I hope one day I'll find what mam and Papà have—what you and Declan have."

"You will. I know it." She smiles at me.

I really hope she's right. I kiss the top of her head, then go to finish getting ready.

We drive to The Legacy, the hotel where the ball is being held. We see all the firefighters and police officers in their Class A uniforms. Heading inside, I can see that they have the ballroom set up in police and firefighter colors—blues and reds with splashes of black and white. It's beautifully done. The ballroom is set up with the dance floor in the middle and tables spread out around it. There's already a few people dancing.

I see Sal waving at someone, so we all follow him. I find myself looking at the most beautiful woman I've ever seen and there's a Zac Efron look-alike touching her. That needs to stop.

Schuyler

We arrive at the hotel and the first person I spot when we get inside is Sal. I chuckle, seeing him wave at me.

"You have an entourage now?" I tease him.

Blaine walks over to us and pulls me to him, then he shakes Sal's hand. I notice one of the guys with Sal glaring at Blaine. Weird.

Sal introduces Blaine and me to his family. I watch Blaine smile at Giovanna and Fiorella, but he glares at the guys until he realizes that they're all part of the Mancini family. Then his attitude changes—real fast. Chickenshit. Then he fangirls over Domenico, Declan, and Cillian. Sure he's a Hawks fan, but I'm the real fan. He's what we call a fair-weather fan. He only likes them when they're winning.

After the introductions, Blaine goes straight to the bar and starts talking to some woman in a skintight dress. Oh, did I not mention that he likes to flirt with women in front of me? He says it's to show me that I'm not the only one that wants him. But there's the minor fact that I don't want him and I wish that he would find someone else.

I stand off to the side and feel someone come up beside me.

"Schuyler," I hear a deep voice say. My body reacts to his voice in a way that it's never reacted to anyone before. I feel it in my soul. And it doesn't hurt that he looks like Superman. No, not Christopher Reeves

Superman, Henry Cavil Superman. And he's got those muscles too. I didn't know men could actually look like that in real life. I wonder if he can fly?

I turn towards him. "Sebastiano." Oh good. At least my voice works.

"Where's your boyfriend?" He says 'boyfriend' like it's offending him to say the word out loud. He looks around and spots Blaine at the bar with that woman. She's smiling at him as he leans in to say something to her. He has his hand on her hip.

I sigh softly. I can feel Sebastiano staring at me. Like his Superman X-Ray vision is in overdrive.

"Who the fuck does he think he is? He has a beautiful woman right here, yet he's over there flirting with that tramp?" He scowls. "Why do you put up with that?"

"They're just talking." I look at my hands and shrug.

He puts his hand under my chin and lifts my head to look at him.

"You deserve to be treated like a queen," he murmurs.

When he touches me, everything else fades away. All I see and hear is him. His voice. His touch. He leans down towards me...

Someone slaps Sebastiano on the back, and it breaks the spell we're under.

We both look up and see Gianluca. I panic and look over at the bar. Thank fuck. He's still occupied with that woman. I step back from Sebastiano so I can slow my breathing down. My heart is racing like I just ran a marathon.

The three of us watch Blaine take the woman out on the dance floor. Sebastiano and Gianluca are both sending death glares at Blaine. Too bad it's not working.

"I told you he's a fucktard and that you need to leave his stupid ass." I shake my head and chuckle, turning to see Cap and Lynn. I hug them both.

"This is my captain, Michael Jeffries and his wife Lynn," I say to Sebastiano and Gianluca.

"Mancini, huh? Enea or Leonardo's boys?" Cap asks.

"Enea's my father and Leonardo is Luca's," Sebastiano answers.

"Your fathers are good men. I've heard about everything they're doing for Chicago."

"Thank you, sir." Sebastiano smiles.

He has such a beautiful smile, it lights up his face and shows off those damn dimples. And his eyes. They sparkle when he looks at me. It's like getting lost in a tropical sea of blues and greens. Oh! And those arms, can arms be sexy? Cause holy shit, his are. I wonder what he looks like wet. Like the scene in the movie where Superman comes out of the ocean all glistening and...Why couldn't I have met him before I met Blaine?

Sal and the others come over to stand with us.

"Let's grab a table," Cap says, leading the way.

"You have an awesome job!" Giovanna smiles.

"Thank you." I blush. "What do you both do?"

"I'm taking time off before finishing med school.

Well, I haven't decided if I actually want to do it now." Giovanna chuckles.

Fiorella snorts and shoulder bumps Giovanna.

"I just graduated from Wildcat and I've started my own fashion line. Nothing as altruistic as my smarty-pants cousin." Fiorella snickers at Giovanna.

"Excuse my cousin. She's um, an odd one," Giovanna teases Fiorella.

Their banter makes me miss Mira. We always have fun when we're together. I wish I didn't have to lie to her. I know she knows that something's wrong, but she never pushes. Plus, she hates Blaine.

"Why don't you want to finish med school?" I ask Giovanna.

Declan O'Reilly comes up and wraps his arms around her. They're adorable. It makes me long to have that. I see Blaine glance over at me while he dances with the woman. He smirks at me and nuzzles the woman's neck. I look away and focus on our group instead.

"Declan and I have a six-month-old son, Rowan. I love being home with him, so I haven't decided if I want to go back yet," she explains. She pulls her phone out and shows me a picture of the cutest baby boy with bright green eyes and dimples.

"He's so handsome!" I exclaim.

"And I've told my wife she doesn't have to go back if she doesn't want to. But I'm selfish like that." He snickers. "Then they can both come to every game and even travel with me. Win-win in my book."

Giovanna is gazing adoringly up at Declan while she listens to him. Fuck, I hate Blaine. I look over at Sebastiano and find him staring back at me.

"Dance with me?" I hear him say and shake my head no.

"I can't. I'm sorry."

He frowns and looks over at Blaine still dancing with that woman.

"Why not? Your boyfriend's an asshole. Who dances with another woman when he has you?"

"It's okay. It's just a dance," I whisper and look down. Looking at him makes me more ashamed that I don't know how to leave Blaine. I know I look like I'm letting him walk all over me.

I want to dance with Sebastiano so fucking bad. To feel those sexy arms around me...but I know if I do that, the consequences later tonight will be horrific. Unless he goes home with that woman. I mean, I can hope, right?

"I'm going to tell that shitbag off if he doesn't get off the fucking dance floor and keep his hands to himself —" Cap snarls. Lynn's nodding and staring daggers at Blaine too.

"Come on Cap, it's fine..." I trail off because the look he's giving me shuts me up pretty fast. I know when not to poke the Cap bear.

Sebastiano grabs my hand and pulls me onto the dance floor anyway. My whole body feels alive when he puts his hands on my hips, my heart beats faster and

I feel like I'm floating. I hear his breathing speed up as we move around the dance floor.

Sebastiano

I need this woman. I don't care that she's involved with that asshole. He's disrespecting her in front of everyone anyway. Every part of me is responding to her and by the look in her eyes? I know she feels it too. Who the fuck does he think he is, anyway? He looks familiar and his name...I think he works for us. I'm going to find out. He sure as fuck doesn't deserve her. And besides, she's mine.

She's the opposite of what I'm usually attracted to. She's about five-seven and has the most beautiful curves. Her eyes are a neon blue that just call out to me. They're framed by dark curly hair that's begging me to wrap my hands in it.

I look down and see a slight mark on her neck. It looks like part of a handprint. If that fucker has put his hands on her, I'll kill him. I need to get to know her so I can find out. She knows Sal. Maybe he can tell me about her.

I lead her off the dance floor when the song ends. But I don't take my hand off her waist. I pull her closer to me.

"Is Blaine hitting you?" I whisper in her ear.

She shakes her head no, but won't look at me when she does. I lift her chin so that she has to look at me.

"Schuyler, is Blaine hitting you?" I ask her again softly. I see the war going on in her blue eyes. That fucker has hurt her, I can see it in her eyes. She needs to tell me. I will end him.

"N-no. H-he's never hurt me," she stutters.

Now I know she's lying; she can't even look me in the eye. He's a dead man. I don't fucking care who he is. He's DEAD. She lets go of me and practically runs towards the restroom.

"Gia, Rella, can you check on Schuyler?"

If there's anyone who can help me, it's my sister and cousin. Maybe she'll open up to them.

"What's wrong?" Gia looks at me.

"I saw a mark on her neck, I think he's hitting her. Maybe she needs a friend?" They're both staring at me and Gia nods.

"We'll try. But I don't think we should push her. Especially because she doesn't know us yet. Maybe we can invite her to lunch?" Rella suggests.

"She's mine." I frown. "I need to know what he's done to her."

"Yours?" Gia's eyes get wide.

"Mine. So please help me, sis. If he's hurting her, I'm going to kill him."

I know they both understand what I mean. Gia has Declan, and Rella has Cillian. And now I'll have Schuyler.

Schuyler

I cannot want Sebastiano. This situation is so fucked up—and Mira, I have to protect Mira. I look at the marks on my neck and see that there's a small spot where the concealer has smudged. Fuck. I pull out my compact and cover it up just before Giovanna and Fiorella walk in.

"Hey, are you okay?" Giovanna asks softly.

"Yeah, I'm okay. Did Sebastiano send you in?"

"Yes, and no. He's worried about you, and from what he said, we are too."

I take a deep breath and look at both of them. I'm not used to having girlfriends who care about what's going on with me anymore. In fact, I don't have any girlfriends anymore. I had some before I met Blaine and after we broke up, I started hanging out with them again. None of them liked Blaine, and they were so happy when I left him. When I went back to him, they kept telling me to leave him, but I kept saying I loved him. I started flaking on lunches and dinners because the abuse was getting worse and I was having a hard time hiding it. We slowly started drifting apart, and eventually they stopped asking all together. I still get random texts, but they don't ask me to come out anymore.

I feel like maybe I can trust Giovanna and Fiorella. That they won't leave me like my other friends did. But

I don't want anything to happen to them just because they know what's going on. Blaine used to threaten my friends. They're Mancinis though…They would be safe from him.

"I'm okay." They're both staring at my neck and chest. I'm silently praying that I didn't miss another spot.

"We were wondering if you'd like to have lunch with us tomorrow? We can go shopping after," Gia says. She's looking at me in the mirror. "Maybe Mira would like to come too? We'd love to meet her."

"I'd like that. I'm off tomorrow so that would be perfect. I'll text Mira and ask her if she wants to come."

I pull my phone out.

> Schuyler: Hey! Are you busy
> tomorrow?

> Mirabelle: Nope. What's going on?

> Schuyler: Met some new friends and
> they invited us to lunch and shopping
> tomorrow. Interested?

> Mirabelle: Who are they?

> Schuyler: Giovanna O'Reilly and
> Fiorella Mancini

> Mirabelle: (shocked emoji) Sure. What
> time? Should I meet you at your
> place?

Schuyler: Do you want to sleep over
tonight? I won't be back for a while.
But you have keys

Mirabelle: Okay I'll come over

Schuyler: Awesome. I'll text you when
I'm on my way home

Mirabelle: Is Blaine coming home
with you?

Schuyler: Not sure. But I'll text
you soon

"What's your schedule like?" Rella asks.

"I work one twenty-four hour day, then two days off. Unless I pick up extra shifts. And Mira said she'd love to join us tomorrow."

I see them nod while I explain.

"Awesome! Give me your phone, I'll put both our numbers in. We can pick you up tomorrow."

"We can SHOP!" Fiorella giggles. Giovanna is shaking her head no.

I snicker. "You don't like to shop?"

"Oh, hell no. I only do it because I have to."

We head out of the restroom together. Gia's adding their numbers into my phone. Then she starts a group chat, so my number goes to their phones too.

"We're going to have so much fun!" Fiorella is twirling around and bumps into Cillian.

I watch them and laugh. Yeah, I definitely want that, and I know I'll never have it with Blaine. I feel arms circling my waist and a scowl appears on Giovanna's face.

"Hey, baby. I was wondering where you went. I met a girl named Shauna. She invited us to an after party," he says as he tightens his hold on me. I can smell perfume on him and I'm doing everything I can not to gag.

"We have plans tomorrow! Schuyler can't stay out late," Fiorella informs Blaine. He just stares at her.

"What plans?" He snaps his head to look at me.

"We're going to lunch," I answer.

"And shopping!" Fiorella smiles.

"We're supposed to hang out with Shauna tomorrow. I already told her we would."

I see Giovanna staring at Blaine. She looks at me, then Fiorella.

"Well, we're really looking forward to having lunch with Schuyler. So, we'd appreciate it if you'd let her come out with us." I think she knows what's going on without me having to tell her.

Blaine takes a deep breath. "I guess we can meet up with Shauna after your little outing."

"Thank you," I murmur.

I look over at Giovanna and Fiorella. They're staring intently at Blaine and me. It's like they're studying us. I can never tell them what goes on. They would try to convince me to leave him. Then how would I make sure he stays away from Mira?

Fiorella claps. "Yay! Lunch and shopping!" She

giggles. Cillian wraps his arms around her and kisses her neck.

I feel Blaine dig his fingers into my side. "We'll discuss this later," he whispers.

I knew him giving in was too good to be true.

Sebastiano

I watch my sister and cousin hover around Schuyler. I know I'm right about that asshole hitting her, but I need to find out the details so that I can help her. He'll rot in hell for hurting her. In fact, I'll be showing him the way there soon. Very soon.

"So, Blaine, what do you do?" I ask the douchebag, keeping eye contact with him while I wait for him to answer.

"I work for your family's company," he replies.

"You do? What department?"

"I'm in marketing. I help with the designs for our marketing campaigns."

Who the fuck does he think he is? 'Our' marketing campaigns? He's not part of the 'our' in the Mancini family. I make a mental note to look into his records.

To him, I nod. "Do you enjoy what you do?"

"I do. I have a great team and so far, all our campaigns are doing well. Also, my father is Conrad Blackwell."

If that asshole thinks throwing his father's name around is going to help, he's sadly mistaken. I don't care who the fuck his father is. I know Conrad, he's on the board of our company. My papà and zios have been trying to kick him off the board for a while now. He thinks that the investments we're doing are illegal. He's been blabbing about it to other board members and to the cops. Everyone knows we're not doing anything illegal when it comes to our company, but he just won't stop.

Detectives come around lately asking questions about our businesses. It's complete bullshit and not even Salvatore can help us because it's not his division.

I've never liked Conrad, and I like his son even less. Seems the apple doesn't fall far from the tree.

I see Schuyler flinch slightly when Blaine puts his arm around her. I want to go over there, rip his arms off and use them to beat the fuck out of him.

I feel my twin nudging me.

"What's going on with you? Since when are you interested in shitbags like him?" he whispers.

"I don't give a fuck about him."

My brother is giving me weird looks and then I see realization forming on his face.

"You like her. Schuyler," he whispers again.

I look at him and nod.

He'll understand once I get to talk to him and explain myself. I can't do it here, not with everyone listening.

Schuyler

After dinner, I lose track of Blaine. Again.

I feel someone come up beside me while I'm looking for him and I know it's Sebastiano. This connection between us is crazy. He leans in towards me.

"You need to leave him," he whispers in my ear.

"Why? He's done nothing wrong." I turn and look up at him. He's looking at me like I've grown a second head.

"Then where is he? Why isn't he here with you?"

I shrug my shoulders. "He's probably in the restroom." The exact moment I say that, we see him stumble out of the restroom with Shauna hanging on him. My face turns bright red and I can feel Sebastiano's eyes boring into me. I don't want to be seen as that dumb woman who saw the cheating and stayed. But that's exactly what I look like right now.

"What the ever-loving fuck?" Sebastiano balls his hands into fists as we watch them.

"Please don't. You don't know the circumstances," I whisper, putting my hand on his arm.

He looks down at me and I can see that he's at war with his anger. He finally takes a deep breath.

"Okay, I'll drop it for now, Schuyler, but you need to tell me what's going on. I need to understand why a beautiful, intelligent woman would let that shitbag walk all over her."

"One day, Sebastiano. But please, not tonight."

I can see the pain in his beautiful blue-green eyes. Then he wraps me in a hug that I melt into.

"You'll be mine soon. And then you won't be able to stop me from finding out the truth," he whispers in my ear.

I step back and look at him. Of course I would love to be in his arms every day. I hate Blaine. It's a mantra I repeat to myself every day.

The night's winding down and again I find myself having to look for Blaine. This is the third time tonight. Cap, Lynn, and all the Mancinis have been by my side all night. It's the best night I've had in a long time.

"Don't forget about tomorrow! Lunch and shopping!" Fiorella reminds me.

I can't help but smile at her. "I won't forget. What time should I be ready?"

"We'll pick you up at ten-thirty. Text me your address," Giovanna says.

I take my phone out to text her, and I see a text from Blaine.

Blaine: Hey baby, I'm going to the club with Shauna. I'll pick you up after your little 'outing' tomorrow. Oh and I took my car. Cap can drop you off, right?

Schuyler: Okay, have fun! I'll talk to you later. And yeah, I'll ask Cap to take me home

Blaine: I love you

Schuyler: Ditto

I smile at my phone, forgetting that I need to text Giovanna.

"Is everything okay?"

I tilt my head to the side and look at Sebastiano.

"Yeah, everything is great. I just need to get an Uber."

"Why do you need an Uber?" Sal asks. He's frowning at me. "Where's McDouchebag?"

"He texted me, he left with Shauna and went to the club he was talking about earlier."

"Wait. He fucking went with that woman and left you here?" Giovanna looks at me while I nod. "Does he live with you?"

"No. He lives in Old Town. I live in Evanston," I explain.

"We'll take you home. You don't need an Uber," Sebastiano says.

I start to say he doesn't need to.

"I wasn't asking," he growls out.

"Let's go to O'Connor's," Sal suggests.

Everyone says okay.

"I should go home," I say.

"Shush. We're going to O'Connor's and you're going to love it," Fiorella says while she links her arm with mine.

"I wouldn't fight her. She's always been this bossy." Gianluca laughs at the look on my face.

I snort. "Okay. I won't fight."

Fiorella cheers, she has a death grip on my arm and I chuckle. It's then that I notice two huge guys behind our group and I can't help staring at them.

"Did you know there's two ginormous, tattooed guys following us?" I whisper to Fiorella while we're walking to the cars.

She laughs. "We forgot to introduce you to them. This is Grady and Marco. They're our bodyguards."

"You have bodyguards? Are we gonna die?" I blurt out.

Everyone laughs.

"No, we're not in danger. But I'm sure you've heard the stories about our family. Well, they're here to make sure no one messes with us. And with Dom, Declan and Cillian being pretty famous here in Chicago, there are people who try to get a little too close. They help keep us safe," she says.

"I would be scared of them too." I giggle.

Grady and Marco both snort when they hear me. I blush. "Sorry. I mean, I'm sure you're nice, but you look super intimidating."

Sebastiano puts his arm around me. "They're big marshmallows."

We all pile into two SUV. I end up sitting between Sebastiano and Sal.

"Have you been to O'Connor's before?" Sal asks.

"No, I don't get out much."

"You're going to love it."

Sebastiano

I can't believe Blaine left Schuyler at the ball. And on top of that? He left with another woman. Who fucking does that? Originally, I was only going to kill him for touching her. Now? I'm going to kill him even slower for cheating on her. I want to claim her right now, to kiss her enticing full lips. But I won't. I won't be the reason she cheats on him. I will be the reason she leaves him.

As we drive, I think of all the ways I'm going to torture Blaine. I get so wrapped up in my thoughts that before I know it, we're parking at O'Connors.

I help Schuyler out of the car and hold on to her hand. She doesn't even try to pull away from me. It's like we're two magnets drawn together.

The bouncers wave us through, and we hear people standing in line talking as we walk by. Some are questioning why we're being let in before them, and some are oohing and aahing at Declan, Cillian and Dom. It always makes me chuckle. Being Dom's identical twin, I get mistaken for him a lot. I feel Schuyler lean into me as she tries to hide from the line of people.

We get inside and find a table that can accommodate all of us. Our regular server comes over and gets our drink order.

"What do you think of O'Connor's?" I've been watching her look around.

"It's pretty cool. I pass by here every time I go to a Panthers game, but I've never come in."

"You're a Panthers fan?" Gianluca perks up.

She chuckles. "I love the Panthers and the Hawks."

"So, who's your favorite Panther?" He grins at her expectantly.

I roll my eyes at my cousin. Gianluca's the third baseman for the Chicago Panthers and he better keep his Panther paws to himself. I pull her closer to me and hold onto her.

"You're my favorite Panther, duh." She laughs.

"YES!" he does a little dance and high-fives her.

I put my nose in her hair, taking a deep breath. "You smell delicious," I whisper in her ear. I feel her shiver slightly and lean into me more. I love how responsive she is to me. She smells like spiced apples and I want to eat her up.

Blaine Blackwell he's a dead man. He touched my girl. He'll never touch another woman like that again. EVER.

I notice Blaine doesn't text her at all while we're out. So, I'm pretty sure he's cheating, or will cheat on her, and that makes me even angrier than I already am. Even if Schuyler was a raging bitch, she doesn't deserve to be treated the way he treats her. Why doesn't he leave her? Why doesn't she leave him? There are so many fucking questions going around in my head that I need answers to.

I watch her smiling and having a good time with my family. It's like she's already a part of us. Gia and Rella seem to like Schuyler already. I love it because that means when the time is right and we're finally together, there won't be that weird 'get to know each other' phase.

Schuyler

"You need to come with us to the next Hawks home game," Gia says. "It's on Tuesday night. And if I remember correctly, you're off that day, right?"

I think about it for a minute. "Yep! I'm off tomorrow, then again on Tuesday and Wednesday."

"Woo! It's a date! Have you been to any Hawks' games?" Rella asks.

"I have, but lately I haven't been able to get to any

games at all. I used to go at least once a month. Sometimes more because Cap is a huge Hawks fan too, so he would go with me." I chuckle. "This season has been awesome."

"Well, now you have us, so you'll go to a lot more games," Rella says.

"Panthers' games too," Gianluca adds in.

I smile at all of them. I wish I could be around them more, but Blaine will never allow it. Or I should say he'll never let me go alone. He'll invite himself if he has to. Times like these make me hope he has a lot of work trips coming up.

Being near Sebastiano calms me. Like there's nothing that can hurt me when he's around. Maybe when I figure out how to leave Blaine, then I can be with Sebastiano. If he doesn't find someone else before I can do it. The thought of him being with someone else makes me nauseous. I see Gia and Rella smiling at me as Sebastiano holds me close. Maybe just for tonight I can forget Blaine and feel what it would be like to be wanted. Truly wanted, and not owned.

Tonight was the most fun I've had in a long time. Being with the Mancinis was exactly how I imagined life could be. Relaxing, fun, lots of laughing and genuine family. I can't wait till tomorrow, I get to spend the whole day with Gia and Rella. I don't even mind the shopping part.

I watch all of them as they joke and laugh with each other. I think Mira would fit in too. She loves to laugh and just have fun. This is the family I wished for as a child. I hope I can find a way to get away from Blaine. Maybe Sebastiano will still be here for me. It's like he knows what I'm thinking as he pulls me closer to him and kisses my head. This must be what heaven feels like. And if it is? I don't ever want to leave.

Sebastiano

Holding Schuyler is everything to me, I never really thought that I would feel this way about someone. I'll be the first to admit that when Gia and Declan met, I didn't understand how they could feel so strongly about each other so fast. I even told Declan to back off numerous times. But I get it now. I know that there's nothing I wouldn't do to keep Schuyler with me. The only thing I need to take care of is Blaine and with the way he treats her, I don't think it's going to be hard to make him go away.

I wish this night could go on forever. I don't want to say good night to Schuyler, she's the first woman that I've wanted to know everything about. And in this short time I've learned so much about her. She loves sports as much as I do, and she wants to travel. Her sister Mira's the most important person to her and I can't wait to meet her. Watching her with my family makes my heart feel full. I've never introduced a woman to my family before, but now I can't wait for her to meet my parents.

I need to figure out how to win her heart without killing Blaine. Or maybe that's the answer. He is a slimy low-life turd that thinks he can put his hands on a woman. My woman. Fuck that.

I hold her tighter while I think of ways to make Blaine disappear. I mean go away. I still can't believe he left Schuyler at the ball and went out with that other woman.

Schuyler

I wake up smiling. Not only did I have a great time with the Mancinis, I woke up alone. I grab my phone and there are no calls or texts from Blaine either. Maybe he really did hook up with Shauna and now he'll leave me. Maybe I could actually be free of him.

I hear Mira walking around in the house and it makes me smile. I've missed her.

Giovanna: Wakey wakey eggs and bakey! (bacon and egg emoji)

Fiorella: Did you just call me bacon or eggs? (thinking emoji)

Giovanna: I'm not sure if there's a right
answer to that…so…You're bacon
(bacon emoji) Skye is the eggs (egg
emoji)

>Fiorella: If I'm the bacon and Skye is
the eggs, wtf are you? And what about
Mira?

Giovanna: I'm the orange juice. DUH.
And Mira…well she's the plate (plate
emoji)

I giggle at their texts coming in.

Giovanna: Are you up, Skye? Are we
picking Mira up at her dorm?

>Schuyler: I'm up! Mira stayed here with
me last night. You two are hilarious
(laughing emoji)

Giovanna: Yay! We'll be picking you
two up in an hour

>Schuyler: Okie dokie! We'll be
waiting

Yawning and stretching, I wince at the pain. I roll over and get out of bed to grab a shower. I take my time covering up my marks and bruises. At least I remembered to ice them last night—it helps them heal faster. It's worked before, but for now, concealer is my best friend.

I get dressed and head into the living room. "Morning, Mouse."

Mirabelle rolls her eyes at me. "I'm way louder than a mouse now."

I laugh. "Maybe, but you'll always be Mouse to me." I make squeaking noises at her and she laughs.

"And you'll always be Squirrel."

I smile at the memory of our nicknames. After what happened with our parents, Mira didn't really talk a whole lot and when she did it sounded more like she was squeaking. So I started calling her Mouse. She says she called me Squirrel because I was always making plans for us to have a better life. Like a squirrel stores nuts away for the winter.

While we're waiting, I hear a text come in. My stomach turns because I know it's Blaine. Fuck.

Blaine: Hi, my love! How was your
night? Did you miss me?

Schuyler: It was good. Came home
and went to bed. How was your night?

Blaine: The club was fucking crazy!
Shauna got us in without having to
wait. I'm sorry I didn't come over after,
I passed out on her couch

I hate him so fucking much. I know he slept with her, and I don't care. I hope he leaves me for her.

"Is that Blaine? Wasn't he at the ball with you last night?" Mira asks me.

I want to lie to her but the look on her face says she'll know.

"Yeah he was with me, but he left with another

woman and went to a club. I stayed with Cap, Mama and the Mancinis."

"Wait. He left you there and went to a club with some woman he just met? What a fucking dickface."

I sigh. "It's fine, Mouse. I had a really good time last night."

She frowns at me but stays quiet. I know she heard us fighting when she lived with me. But I hope she doesn't know about the abuse. I've done my best to hide it from her. I don't want her to feel like it's her fault or that she has to help me fix this situation.

> Schuyler: It's okay, Mira came over last night and we hung out. Shauna seems like a cool person

>> Blaine: Are you jealous, baby? Why would Mira come over? You could've just called me if you were lonely

> Schuyler: No, not jealous. And Mira just wanted to hang out

>> Blaine: Don't forget, you're my girl. FOREVER. I'll see you tonight. I love you

I wince when I see that. I need out. Fuck, I can't do this. I feel like I'm dying slowly. Maybe if I tell Gia and Rella? No! I can't bring them into this. It's not their fight, it's mine and mine alone.

I hear a knock at the door, and I walk over to answer it. I get a double hug from Gia and Rella. This family likes to hug. A lot.

"Oh my god you're adorable!" Fiorella yells and lunges for Mira.

Mira doesn't move fast enough and she's engulfed by Fiorellas hug. I can hear her giggling.

'I'm Fiorella. I'm the fun Mancini. That's Giovanna—she's the unfun Mancini."

"Mancini-O'Reilly," Gia corrects her.

Rella snorts. "See? Un. Fun."

"Are you guys ready?" Gia asks. She looks around my apartment. "He's not here, is he?"

"Who? Oh, you mean Blaine? Nope. He never came over last night. In fact, I just heard from him while I was waiting for you two."

Gia gives me a sad look. "Can I ask you something, Skye?"

"Of course."

"Why are you with him? He clearly doesn't respect you. He left with another woman he claims he just met at the party and then he didn't text you until ten-thirty the next morning. Did he go home?"

Mira is nodding at Gia while she talks.

"I hate Blaine," she says. "He's not right for Squirrel."

"Squirrel?" Rella giggles.

"She's Mouse, I'm Squirrel," I explain while I try to think up a lie about Blaine. But the look on both their faces tell me they wouldn't believe me any more than Mira would. So, I show them his texts instead.

"Mother...what the fuck?" Rella exclaims. "He 'slept on her couch'? Okay, babygirl. I know we just met you, but we care about you. You need to leave this bastard."

"We can help you if he's hurting you," Gia whispers to me as she hugs me again.

See? There's the hugging again. If they keep this up, I'm going to cry.

"H-he's not a bad person and I love him," I whisper back. "I believe him when he says that he slept on her couch. I'm okay. Really, I am."

The more I talk, the more I feel like I'm trying to convince myself. All three of them are looking at me like they know I'm full of shit. Dammit.

"Aww crap," Mira says right as we're stepping out the door.

"What's wrong?" I ask her.

"My damn study group wants to meet up. We were supposed to meet tomorrow night, but one of them can't do it and everyone else is free today." She's frowning and texting back. She sighs. "I'm so sorry, I'm gonna have to bail on you."

"It's okay, Mouse. School comes first." I hug her.

"You need to come with us Tuesday night to the Hawks game. And we'll definitely do more lunches." Gia smiles.

"I would love to join you for a Hawks game!" She claps with delight. "Thank you so much."

They both hug Mira and we watch her leave. Then we get into Gia's car to get lunch.

Giovanna

Fuck. We need Skye to admit to what that fucking asshole is doing to her. Otherwise, we can't help her. She doesn't seem scared of him, but I know for a fact that she doesn't love him like she says. And he 'says he slept' on that tramp's couch? No fucking way. I would rip Declan's balls off if he 'slept' on another woman's couch.

"I hope that you'll trust us enough one day to tell us what's really going on. You're not alone, Skye. You have the entire Mancini family behind you."

If there's anything that I've learned from school, it's that we can't force her. She has to come to us—she has to be ready to get away from him and to make the change.

So that's what we'll do. We'll surround her with love and support, and hope that she'll open up to us before it's too late. And when I say 'too late'? I mean either Blaine is going to severely hurt her—, maybe even kill her—or my brother Sebastiano's going to kill Blaine. Personally, I think the latter will happen first.

Watching my brother with Schuyler last night...I've never seen him like that with a woman. And he called her his girl. He's found his penguin, and she's with an abusive asshole. But we'll help him save her. That's what we Mancinis do. We help each other.

Schuyler

I tell them all about Mirabelle and how proud I am of her.

"Where are your parents?" Rella asks while we're waiting for our food.

"Our parents died when I was seven, and Mira was two. We grew up in foster care."

"Oh my god. I'm so sorry, Skye." She puts her hand over mine. I didn't even realize my hand was shaking till she did that.

"It's okay. My parents loved the high more than they loved us. I was at school when it happened. Mira was in the apartment when my father shot my mother. Then he turned the gun on himself. The police think that he forgot Mira was there. She was lucky because he probably would've killed her too," I explain in a soft voice.

Now I'm afraid to look at them because I don't want to see pity on their faces. I don't even know why I told them that. I've never told anyone that story, not even Cap or Lynn. Hell, Blaine doesn't even know.

"You're so damn strong," I hear Gia say. I slowly turn to look at her. "Mira is a wonderful woman and I know it's because of you."

I don't see pity on either of their faces. Incredibly, I see love. The kind of love I've only seen from Mira,

Lynn and Cap. I hold back my tears and take a deep breath.

"I'm not really that strong. I just knew I had to take care of Mira and we had an awesome social worker. She made sure they didn't split us up. And she even helped me get guardianship of Mira when I turned eighteen."

"Well, what I said before was true then, and it's even truer now. You're not alone anymore. You have the entire Mancini family and we don't let go easily," Gia says. She puts her hand over Rella's.

"It's great to have two more girls in the family." Rella smiles. Gia's grinning at us. "The boys are always outnumbering us."

"So, what made you want to be a firefighter?" Gia asks.

"Honestly? When my dad killed my mom, I only remember the police officers and firefighters. I told myself that I wanted to help other kids like me. When I got older, I looked into social work, but it would take years of school. I didn't have the time or money for college because I had to take care of Mira. I took the firefighters test, and I told myself if I passed, then that's what I would be."

"That's like why I went into medicine," Gia says. "I wanted to help people."

"Do you think you'll go back and finish your med school?" I ask while we eat.

Gia shrugs. "I don't know. I think I will because I do want to finish what I started. But the thought of being away from Rowan so much makes me sad. The hours are insane, and I would miss out on so much. And we want more babies."

I feel like we all understand each other on a level that I've never experienced with other friends. Like they might actually get why I haven't left Blaine. But I still can't tell them.

I feel my phone buzzing and my stomach drops.

> Blaine: Hey baby, is your little 'outing'
> over yet? Are you home?

"Sorry, I have to answer him real quick." They both nod, but don't take their eyes off me.

> Schuyler: We just started eating and
> we haven't gone shopping yet. I
> probably won't be home until this
> afternoon. Don't worry, go relax and I'll
> see you later

> > Blaine: WTF. You're choosing to spend
> > time with them instead of me? You
> > don't even know them

> Schuyler: They're nice and I'm
> enjoying being around them

> > Blaine: Fine. I'll go see Shauna by
> > myself

I know he thinks that's going to get me mad or jealous. Haha.

Schuyler: Okay. Have fun and tell her I
said hello!

Blaine: We need to talk. TONIGHT

I frown as I read his last text.

Schuyler: Okay. I'll text you later

I put my phone away and give them a smile.

"Is everything okay?" Rella asks.

"Everything's fine. Blaine wanted to know if we were finished. I told him we just started so we probably won't be done until this afternoon."

They both give me huge smiles. I smile back at them and we all start laughing.

"Great! We have lots of shopping to do!" Rella says as Gia rolls her eyes.

We finish eating and drive to the Outlet Mall of Chicago. It's such a huge mall that you could walk around all day and still have more to see. I chuckle at Grady and Marco following us, holding Gia and Rella's bags.

"Makes shopping easier." Rella giggles at Marco while he makes faces at her.

The guys both squint at me because I'm snickering. I can't help it! These are two enormous men that would scare the shit out of any normal person. But here they are walking around with the three girls, carrying our bags. Snicker.

When we get back to my house, the girls come

inside with me. Grady and Marco take a look around the property, then join us inside. I'm guessing they're making sure nothing suspicious is going on out there.

I offer all of them something to drink. Grady and Marco take water. Gia and Rella take some juice.

"Thank you so much for today. I had such a great time," I say to them as we sit and drink.

"Wait till Tuesday. We're going to have so much fun at the game! You'll get to meet our parents and Rowan." Gia beams.

"I can't wait." I smile.

"Do you have plans for tonight? Would you like to come and have dinner with us?" Gia asks.

"Thanks, but I have to be up at three in the morning. My shift starts at four."

"Ew." Rella laughs. "That's way too early."

I laugh along with Gia and Rella. I love being around them. I won't let Blaine take this from me.

"Okay, I hate to leave but I have to get home. It's practice day for the guys so I need to be home for Rowan."

I stand up to walk them to the door. "Thank you again for today."

They surround me in a hug, and I hug them both back. I'm beginning to like all this hugging.

"Don't forget, Tuesday is game day. We'll pick you up at four, the game starts at seven. You can take a tour of the locker room, then decide if you want to watch from our suite or from our seats. We have the whole first row in the two-hundred level, center ice. We'll text you tomorrow, we text everyone every day." Gia chuckles.

"I can't wait." I smile. "You can text me anytime. When I'm on duty, I can talk as long as we're not in the middle of a call."

"You be safe Skye, and don't forget if you need anything—anything—just call us. We'll be here day or night." Rella says.

I can't stop smiling as I gather the ingredients to make my dinner. I'm so glad I met all of them last night. While I'm frying the meat for my tacos, I hear my phone go off.

> Giovanna: (sends a pic of Rowan smiling) Someone wanted to say hi to his newest aunty (green heart emoji)

My heart melts when I read Gia's text.

> Schuyler: He's so adorable. I'm honored to be his aunty (green heart emoji)

> Giovanna: I can't wait for you to meet him. He's going to love you. What are you doing?

> Schuyler: I can't wait either! I'm making dinner

> Giovanna: OHHHH. What's for dinner?

> Schuyler: TACOS!! (taco emoji)

> Giovanna: UGH. Now I want tacos.
> Dammit (tongue emoji)

I snort.

> Schuyler: Come get some (cheesy
> smile emoji)

> Giovanna: Don't tempt me. I will load
> Rowan into the car and come over
> there

I send her a pic of the finished tacos.

> Schuyler: I have extra

> Giovanna: If Declan wasn't bringing
> food home I would totally be there.
> That looks fucking delicious. It's
> settled, tacos for our next girls day

> Schuyler: Sounds good to me (smiley
> emoji)

> Giovanna: Declan just got home. Eat
> lots of tacos (green heart emoji)

> Schuyler: I will. Have a good night
> (green heart emoji)

I turn the TV on and find a movie to watch as I eat my dinner. My thoughts keep going back to Sebastiano. What's he doing? Is he with someone? Is he thinking of me? Cause I can't stop thinking about him.

Chapter Five

Sebastiano

I hope Schuyler's having a good time with Gia and Rella. It's taking everything in me not to text Gia to ask how it's going. After we got home last night, I told Dom and Enzo how I felt about Schuyler. They weren't surprised and said they'll do whatever it takes to help me get my girl. They could tell there's something going on with Schuyler too. But she seemed to relax while we were at O'Connors.

I also did some digging about Blaine and his dad. Blaine is the low man in his marketing group and his dad Conrad used to work for us but now he's an investor and board member. I need to talk to my Zio Leo and see what he has to say about Conrad. I think I'll call him now. Patience was never my strong suit.

"Hey, Bastian."

"Hey, Zio, I wanted to ask you a few questions if you have a sec."

"Of course, what's up?"

"Conrad Blackwell. What kind of guy is he?"

"Conrad? He's a dick. Why? What's going on?"

"He has a son, Blaine. I met him last night with his girlfriend at the Police and Firefighters Ball. I think he's abusing her."

"What the fuck? How do you know? Did she tell you that? I met his son a few times. In fact, he works for us in marketing. We gave him a chance because Conrad asked us to. This was before he became unhinged and started causing problems."

"She didn't say anything, but I saw a bruise on her neck, and it looked like a handprint. That and the way he treats her, I don't like it. He left to go to a club with a woman he claimed to have met at the ball and just left

Schuyler there by herself. Even if he's not abusing her, he's a cheating bastard. He made it a point last night to tell me that he worked for us."

"Well, if she won't admit to the abuse, what do you think you can do? And if he's a cheater...is it really your place to do something about it?"

"I want him to disappear. He's an asshole, Zio. I want to know if it's worth talking to Conrad about him."

"I'll be honest, Bastian. I used to think Conrad was a good man, but lately I've seen him at company functions with other women. I asked him once where Monica— his wife—was and he said she wasn't feeling well so she stayed home."

"Do you think he's abusing his wife too? Or is he just a cheater?"

"I don't know. But his son is everything to him, and I doubt he'll help you with Blaine. He'll back his son even if he's wrong."

"Shit. So, what do I do? I can't stand that he's hurting Schuyler."

"Again, why are you so concerned with this girl?"

"She's mine. I need to get her away from him."

"Whoa. Yours? Are you sure?"

"I've never been more sure of anything ever."

"Dammit. Okay. Let me think about it and I'll get back to you. Don't do anything stupid. We'll get her away from him. I promise you."

"Thank you, Zio. I'm going to talk to Papà too. He needs to know what kind of asshole we have working for us."

"I agree. Why don't we all sit down. You, your papà, Tonio and me. Let's do it tomorrow at lunchtime at your parents' house. I'll call Tonio and we'll be there around twelve."

"Okay. Grazie, Zio. I'll see you tomorrow."

After I hang up with my zio, I feel a little better. If there's one thing I know for sure about my family, we always have each other's backs. I can't wait to have Schuyler in my arms.

I get up and get dressed, then text my papà to let him know about tomorrow and to tell him about Schuyler. I also want to know what he thinks about Conrad and Blaine.

Sebastiano: Hey Papà, where are you?
Are you busy?

Enea: I'm in my office, never too busy
for you. Bring snacks

I snort when I read his text.

Sebastiano: On my way with snacks.
Be there in a couple of hours. Traffic
looks normal

Enea: Okay, figlio. Drive safe. See
you soon

I get in my Corvette Stingray and put the top down —I love days like this. I head to the store to get some snacks and then to my parents' house. I love going home, but sometimes I wish it wasn't such a long drive.

When I get to the house, I see my mam in the kitchen and go over to her.

"Hi, Mam." I kiss her cheek and give her a hug.

"HI, amore. What brings you home today?" she asks. I love hearing my mam speak.

My mam was born and raised in Galway, Ireland and she still has her Irish accent. She's the most beautiful woman inside and out. Dom, Enzo and I got her blue-green eyes, and all four of us got her curly auburn hair. When we were little, she started to teach us her native Gaelic. After Enzo and Gia were taken, she didn't speak her language as much. When she did start interacting with us again, she spoke more Italian than Gaelic. I think it reminded her too much of them to speak it.

"I need to talk to Papà." I show her the snacks and she laughs.

"Did something happen?"

"No. Well, kind of. I met someone last night, her name is Schuyler Viñales. I think her boyfriend is abusing her and he works for us. His name is Blaine Blackwell, Conrad Blackwell is his father."

"I've met Conrad, and his wife Monica. He's not a nice man, and I'm not surprised that his figlio is just like him. Every time I've been around Conrad's wife, she always looked like she was terrified of him. It's really sad."

I nod as I listen to her.

"I think I saw a handprint on Schuyler's neck. But she won't admit that he's hitting her." I frown.

"You like this girl?" She looks up at me.

"I do, Mam. She's the one for me. The only one."

My mam hugs me.

"Then she's a lucky girl to have you on her side. You'll figure out how to help her. I'm sure your papà is waiting for these snacks. I'll be here when you need me."

"Grazie, Mam." I hug her tight. She always seems to know just what to say to make me feel better.

I head to my papà's office. Declan calls it his super-secret Bat Cave. It's pretty cool—you can't see the door unless you know where to look. When Dom and I were little, we used to make it a game to see who could find the door the fastest.

I knock and hear my papà say to come in. I press the spot on the wall that opens the sliding door.

"Hey, Papà." I put the snacks and drinks down on his desk. He stands up and comes around to give me a hug.

"Are you ok, Bastian?"

I hug him back and sigh, then go over and sit on the couch. I tell him everything that's happened so far with Schuyler.

"You're sure this is the woman for you? This fight won't be an easy one. Conrad's a bastard—Tonio and I have been trying to get him voted off the board for a while now. And you know what he's trying to do. You also know how I feel about men who mistreat their women. Your mam has told me what she thinks of Conrad, and I've watched him with other women too.

To hear you say his figlio is just as bad or worse than him makes me angry. Have you asked yourself why she hasn't left him? Is he blackmailing her? Or does she truly love him?"

"Sí, Papà. Schuyler's the one for me and I'll do anything to protect her. I've tried to figure out what he could have on her, but I can't think of anything. I don't think she loves him. I do think he's blackmailing her, though."

He nods at me. "Okay, figlio. Tomorrow we will sit down with your zios and see what we can do to help her."

"Grazie, Papà. I can't wait for you to meet her. She went out with Gia and Rella today. I'm waiting for Gia to text or call to let me know how it went. Her sister was supposed to go with them too."

My papà laughs. "They got your sister to go shopping?"

I laugh with him. "They did. If it's okay, I think I'll stay over tonight since we're meeting here tomorrow."

"Of course. You know we love having you home."

I spend the night hanging out with my parents and texting with Gia. She said they had a great time with Schuyler. Mira was there and they got to meet her, but she had to leave to meet up with her study group for school. Gia thinks I'm right and Blaine is abusing Schuyler. She told me how Blaine texted Schuyler telling her about him hanging out with that woman he left the ball with and how he 'slept' on her couch. It's taking everything in me not to go to Schuyler immediately and bring her home with me then making sure Blaine disappears from her life for good.

Our family may not be criminals anymore, but there are still things that need to be taken care of.

One thing I do know is Blaine will suffer for everything he's done to my Schuyler.

I text her.

> Sebastiano: Hey, gorgeous. I heard you had a good day with Gia and Rella (smiley emoji)

> Schuyler: Sebastiano?

> Sebastiano: Yes. LOL. Who else would know about your day with the girls?

> Schuyler: LOL. How did you get my number?

> Sebastiano: I bribed Gia. Please don't be mad at her.

> Schuyler: I'm not mad. And we had the best day. What are you doing tonight?

> Sebastiano: I came to visit my parents and decided to stay over. What are you doing?

> Schuyler: Where do your parents live? I'm just relaxing, heading to bed soon. I have to be at the station at 4 a.m.

Sebastiano: My parents live in Lake Renegade Township, it's about 2 hours northwest of the city. Holy crap that's early! Can I come and visit you at your firehouse?

Schuyler: Um. Sure. We're always there unless we get a call. You can text me or just come by. I'm on shift till 4 a.m. Tuesday

Sebastiano: I'll definitely come by and see you. Probably around 4 p.m. I'll bring you dinner. Should I bring enough for the guys you work with?

Schuyler: You don't have to bring food

Sebastiano: Well I wasn't asking. (tongue emoji) I'll bring pizza. Everyone loves pizza

Schuyler: Okay. And yes, the guys like pizza. There's only three of us on shift. Cap, Anthony, and me. I hate to cut this short, but I have to get to bed

Sebastiano: Okay, amore. I will text you tomorrow. Sweet dreams, cuore mio

Schuyler: What does cuore mio mean?

Sebastiano: My heart

Schuyler: (red heart emoji)

Schuyler

Sebastiano called me his heart. I wish I could be with him, he makes me feel so safe. But that can never happen, no matter how much I want it. I know he doesn't understand why, but I don't want him involved in this. This is my fight, one that I hope I'll win. Fucking Blaine. I never heard back from him after he said he was going to that woman's house. Even though he said we needed to 'talk'. Not that I'm complaining, I'm glad he didn't come over.

I head to my room and turn the TV on. I'm in the mood for a romantic movie. I put one on while I get ready for bed. If only my life was like a movie. Meet the perfect man, fall in love, spend the rest of our lives together. Sebastiano...If only it worked like that in real life.

Sebastiano

After texting with Schuyler earlier tonight, I decided to surprise her and take her to work in the morning. Not only did I get Schuyler's number from Gia, I also got her address. It should take me an hour and a half to get to her place, maybe two. Either way, I plan to get there at about three in the morning. She only lives five minutes from my home in Evanston. But since I stayed at my parent's house, I'll make the drive to see her.

I know that Blaine could be there when I show up. But chances are he won't be, since she didn't say he was there when we were texting. And if he is, then I'll just head back to my parents.

I set my alarm for twelve-thirty and lie down to take a nap.

Chapter Six

Schuyler

I was dreaming about Sebastiano, and we were on a camping trip. Everyone was there, including Cap and Mama. Just as I was about to kiss Sebastiano, I'm jolted awake by a hand over my mouth and another around my neck. I try to move, but whoever it is has me pinned down. They stuff something in my mouth and duct tape over it. Then they tie my hands to my headboard. My brain finally processes what's happening and my vision starts to focus. I see the outline of a person...and realize it's Blaine.

"You thought you could just do whatever the fuck you? Blow me off for those Mancini assholes?" he slurs.

Fuck me, he's wasted...How the fuck did he get into

my house? He doesn't have a key and I don't leave one out anywhere.

"I'll teach you what happens when you do this shit to me. And next time? Mira will learn too—because of you," he cackles.

I hear myself whimper at the mention of my sister.

"My father was right about you. He said you would be a fucking pain in my ass. All you do is fuck everything up."

I can understand most of what Blaine is spewing at me. But he's also slurring so much that there's parts I don't get. I stay quiet, letting him ramble on. Maybe he'll get tired and pass out.

"Those fucking Mancini pieces of shit. My father helped fund them when they were getting their so-called legitimate businesses started. But they'll never be anything but criminals, we know they're still dirty and been working with other mafias. That's how they got all those fucking properties. And that's who you want to fuck now? Stupid bitch." He punches me in the stomach as spittle rains down on me. "Now they want to kick my father off the board because he knows too much. They'll see what happens when they fuck with the Blackwells. They think because they're mafia they can do whatever they want. Fuck that. We will take what's ours. Starting with your dumb ass. I will ruin you. And then no one will want you."

I can feel him grinding on me and he's moaning in my ear. Now I'm starting to panic. He's never forced himself on me before but with the state he's in? I don't know what he'll do and as hard as I try, I can't stop the lone tear that slips down my face. He smirks at me as he rips my nightshirt open and starts to pull my shorts down.

I keep trying to get out from under him but because my hands are tied, all I can do is try to buck him off me. I finally get one of my legs between his and kick upwards. He falls to the side clutching his balls.

"You fucking bitch! I was going to take my time with you. But now? Fuck that. I'm going to make sure you suffer and when I'm done, I'll get Mira and do the same to her." He lunges towards at me, and I try to dodge him, but I'm not fast enough. He punches me with a closed fist and I gasp at the pain exploding across my face. He's never hit me in the face before. For once I'm afraid that he's lost it. If he's willing to mark my face...

He continues to hit me and I think I blackout a few times. When I come to this time, I'm on the ground and he's stalking over to me. I can feel the blood dripping down the side of my head, into my eyes. I take a second to try and blink the blood out of my eyes. That's all it takes for him to be right in front of me. He laughs menacingly. "You stupid whore, you're fucking worthless. You should know that Shauna's a good fuck, she's ten times better than you've ever been. We've been seeing each other for the past three months. Now I just need you to disappear so that I can be the grieving boyfriend, and she will be there to comfort me. My life will be perfect."

I make a noise that was supposed to be a snort. But it comes out sounding more like a wheezing sound as he rips the gag out of my mouth. "I don't care who you've been fucking."

He stares at me then swings again, but misses. "You're too much of a gutless bitch to leave me. I know you've been with Salvatore, you cheating slut. And I saw you with Sebastiano Mancini. You think I didn't see the way you looked at him? He's a fucking player. I treat you like a fucking queen!" He slaps me as he shouts. "I bet you fucked him and all his brothers the night of the ball."

He turns and stumbles away from me. I'm trying to move slowly so that he doesn't notice me reaching for the gun I keep under my nightstand.

Anger bubbles up inside me when he calls me worthless and then a gutless bitch. "Sebastiano is more of a man than you'll ever be. And so is Salvatore. You? You're the worthless fuck, not me," I spit out. "Sebastiano makes me feel everything you can't."

I know I shouldn't have said that last sentence...

He spins around to look at me, his face a mask of rage. Suddenly, he charges me. "You won't fucking shoot me."

I lift my trembling arms, point the gun at him and pull the trigger, fighting to keep from blacking out.

Sebastiano

I can't stop smiling on the drive to Schuyler's house. Traffic is unusually good and I make it to her house earlier than I expected. As I slow down and pull into her driveway, I see a car parked kind of sideways on it. I frown, turn my car off and debate whether I should knock. If that's Blaine's car, I could make this really bad for my girl.

I sit in my car and grapple with my feelings on going in. Finally I sigh. Fuck it, I decide to take the chance and get out of my car. Just as I'm about to knock, I hear a single gunshot. I don't see any lights on inside and none of her neighbors seem to have heard it. I kick in the door and call for her.

"Schuyler! It's Sebastiano!"

"You dumb bitch! You fucking shot me!"

I hear someone yell. I'm guessing it's Blaine; I follow his voice and see them on the floor. Schuyler is pointing a gun at him and he's clutching his side. I run over to Schuyler. She's shaking and has blood all over her. She looks like she's going to pass out at any moment.

"Baby. Give me the gun. It's okay," I say softly to her. It takes a minute but she finally looks at me.

"S-sebastiano? W-what are you d-doing here?" she stutters out.

I gently put my hands over hers and take the gun out of her hands. I put the safety on, slip it into my waistband and gather her in my arms. I shift her slightly so that I can keep an eye on Blaine. She lets out a small whimper when I move her and the rage inside me doubles.

"What did he do to you?" I grit my teeth and ask her as calmly as I can.

"She's a fucking whore and deserved everything she got!" Blaine yells. He's coughing and spitting out blood. "Call an ambulance you, fucking moron! That slut's going to jail."

If I wasn't so worried about Schuyler, I would go over and shoot him myself till I was sure he was fucking dead. As it is, I need to call my papà and get help some with this situation. There's no fucking way my girl is going to go down for shooting this shitbag punk.

I pull my cell out and call my papà.

"Bastian? Why are you calling? What's going on?" my papà answers, sounding confused.

I quickly explain what happened. I can hear him getting up and getting dressed. In the background I can hear my mam asking what's wrong. He explains it to her and she says she's coming too.

"I'm calling your zios. Text me Schuyler's address, we'll be there as soon as we can. I can hear that bastard. Make sure he doesn't cause the neighbors to call the police. Do you think they heard the gunshot?"

"I don't know. I didn't see any lights come on."

"Okay. I'm calling Sal too. We'll need his help with this. Take care of your girl. See you soon, figlio."

I hang up then text Schuyler's address to my papà. Then I look over at Blaine. "What kind of pussy attacks a woman?"

He snorts. "She's not a woman, she's a fucking cow."

I finally notice the alcohol smell rolling off him in waves, and he's slurring. I hear a strangled sob coming from Schuyler. I stand up and go find something to try to clean her up. I need to see what kind of damage he's done to her.

"Please," she begs. "D-don't go."

My heart breaks hearing her beg. "I'm not going anywhere, cuore mio. I need to get something to clean you up with so I can see what he's done to you."

Schuyler looks over at Blaine. I can see the questions in her face that she wants to ask him. I think this is the worst he's done to her, but I can't be sure until I'm able to talk to her. Either way, he's a dead man. I get up and go into her bathroom, grab a towel and get part of it wet, still keeping an eye on Blaine in case he gets any stupid ideas.

Schuyler

I shot Blaine. Holy shit, Mira! Who's going to take care of her when I go to jail? A sob escapes me, thinking of my sister. I don't know why Sebastiano's here, but I'm so grateful that he is. I can see the anger at Blaine on his face and he's not hiding how he feels about me either. I watch Blaine watching us and he's got the ugliest look on his face.

"So you and Sebastiano, huh? I knew it, I knew you were a whore. You fucking bitch."

Before I can answer, Sebastiano comes charging out of the bathroom and gets in Blaine's face.

Sebastiano

"Don't you ever call Schuyler a whore or a bitch or anything else but her fucking name. You're lucky that you're still fucking breathing. Savor it because you won't be for long." I keep my voice low and I see terror settling into his features.

"You wouldn't dare kill me. M-my father will bring hell down on you fucking Mancinis if you hurt me. I'm a Blackwell," he says, but his voice falters.

I snort. "Do you really think your father has the balls to go up against mine? Think again, asshole. No one is so stupid as to think they can win against Enea Mancini."

His eyes get even wider, and he's sputtering while trying to sit up.

I go back over to Schuyler and start to gently clean her face. "I can call Gia to come and help. You need to go to the hospital," I whisper to her gently.

"N-no hospital. Please," she begs.

"Did he rape you?" I ask her, trying to keep my voice steady. I'm looking at her clothes or should I say the lack of clothes while I ask this. I don't know if I could hold myself back if he did.

"N-no. He tried but I got him off me b-before he could, I think. I blacked out a few times."

I pray that he didn't touch her when she blacked out. Now I know she has to be looked at. Gia can help. "And Gia? Are you okay if I call her?"

I see her nod and pull out my phone to make the call.

"Hullo? Bastian? What's wrong?"

Gia answers groggily.

"Gia, I'm so sorry to wake you. I need you to come to Schuyler's house. Right now. Please."

I hear her getting up and Declan asking what's

wrong. She tells him she doesn't know, but she has to get to Schuyler's and asks him to talk to me.

"What's going on?"

I explain to him as fast as I can.

"I'm so sorry, Declan. But I need Gia."

"Okay, Bastian. She's coming. Call me if you need anything."

"Thank you."

As I gently try to clean up some of the blood on her face, she whimpers softly. I hear Blaine snickering. I stand up and just as I'm about to go take a step towards him, I get a text.

> Giovanna: I'm here

> Sebastiano: Door should be open. I kicked it in when I got here

> Giovanna: I see that. At least you didn't break it

"Last door on the left," I call out so that Gia can hear me.

Gia steps into the room with Grady and looks around.

"What the fuck," she says under her breath as she walks over to Schuyler.

Grady's taking up the whole doorway, staring at Blaine. Blaine's eyes look like they're going to pop out of his ugly face.

I hold Schuyler while Gia looks her over and carefully cleans her up.

"I really think that you should go and get checked out," she says to Schuyler.

"No. No hospital," she says adamantly.

"You could have internal trauma," Gia pleads with her.

"Cuore mio, please go with Gia to the hospital. I'll never forgive myself if something is wrong and we could've fixed it. Now that I have you, I can't lose you." I kiss her head. It takes a few minutes but she finally agrees.

"I'll stay with you the whole time. They know me at Evanston Memorial and if you need more care, I'll have you transported to Lucciola Memorial," Gia explains.

"Why Lucciola Memorial?" Schuyler asks.

"It's in our hometown. I can do more for you there."

"Okay. W-what about him?" she gestures weakly at Blaine.

"Don't you worry about him, cuore mio. In fact, you won't have to worry about him ever again." I hold her while she cries softly. "You're mine now."

I pick Schuyler up and carry her to Gia's car while

Grady stays in the room to keep an eye on shitbrick. I place her gently in the front seat and strap her in.

"Gia will keep me updated. I'll come to you after we take care of Blaine."

"Thank you. I don't know why you came, but thank you," she whispers.

"I'll always be here from now on. You're mine, Schuyler, and I'm going to do everything I can to protect you." I carefully wipe the tears on her cheeks and kiss her forehead, "You're cuore mio. My heart." When I don't feel her pull away, I know she's hearing me. I have to go back. "I'll see you soon, cuore mio."

I can hear Schuyler quietly sobbing. It's killing me to leave her, but I need to take care of Blaine. I hug Gia before she gets into the car. "Holy shit, Bastian," she gasps as she hugs me back.

I take a few deep breaths; I can't break down now. Later maybe, but not now.

"Please take care of her, Gia. I can't lose her. And make sure they do a rape kit. She's not sure if he did or not," I whisper to her.

"I will. I won't let her out of my sight. I promise."

I hug my sister one more time and I go back into the room so that Grady can drive them to the hospital. I give Grady a hug as he steps out of the room.

"Take care of them both, please."

"Of course, Bastian," he responds.

I go back into the room and stare at Blaine. He's a lot paler than when I first saw him.

"You really think no one heard the fucking gun go

off?" He laughs. "That bitch is going to jail. I'm going to make sure everyone knows what she did."

"How are you planning on doing that if you're dead?"

He scoffs. "You won't kill me. You don't have it in you. I saw the way you looked at Skye at the ball. She got what she deserved and it's your fault."

I stay quiet while I listen to him. He's fucking crazy and this world will be better without him in it. But he's wrong about one thing—I don't care if he dies.

Zio Leonardo: Tonio and I are here, we're coming in. Your papà and mam are still on the road

Sebastiano: Door's unlocked. Last bedroom down the hallway

I look up and see my zios coming into the room.

"Well, you don't look so good," my Zio Antonio says to Blaine.

"Aren't, you the smart one," he slurs out. "Fucking genius."

Both of my zios laugh at Blaine.

"Maybe if he was sober, he would see the dire situation he's in. Then again, maybe not. He seems like he's as stupid as his father." Zio Antonio snorts.

"My father is going to take you all down," he mumbles.

"Jesus, he's drunk? All this blood is his?" Zio Tonio asks.

"No. the blood here is Schuyler's. Fuckwad's blood

is only on him as far as I can tell."

My zio Leo gets on his phone as he leaves the room.

Blaine starts fumbling for his phone, but Zio Tonio takes it from him.

"Hey! I need a fucking ambulance. Give me my phone back."

Uncle Tonio ignores Blaine. "What kind of asshole beats a woman?"

"Skye's a slut. I shoulda beat her more often. Like an animal. She never learned her fucking lesson, she was always fucking other men. I know she was fucking Sal and Sebastiano, at least now she knows I was fucking Shauna."

I stalk over to him with every intention of making sure he can never say another word about my Schuyler again. But before I can get to the fucker, my zio stops me.

"Don't touch him. We're taking care of it," he says quietly to me.

I frown as I listen to my zio. "I can't just walk away, he hurt my girl. And he can't get away with saying that shit about her."

"I know, Bastian, but you need to let us handle this from here on out. Your job now is to take care of your girl. Blaine won't be a problem anymore, go to Schuyler."

I slowly nod while glaring at Blaine. I know I should listen to my zio but I want to kill Blaine with my bare hands, not leave it to someone else. It's my job to make sure he's never able to hurt Schuyler again. But I know I have to trust my papà and zios to take care of things right now.

My papà and mam finally join us in the room. My mam pulls me into a hug.

"Where's Schuyler?" Mam asks.

"Gia took her to the hospital. I stayed here to make sure Blaine didn't do anything stupid."

I look at my hands and see Schuylers blood on them. I hold in a sob and head into the bathroom to wash it off.

My mam gets on the phone with Gia to check up on them.

"You should take your mam and go to the hospital," my papà says softly. He starts to lead my mam and me out of the room.

"What are you going to do with him? I need to—"

"We're just going to make sure he understands that he's never to come near Schuyler again. And if he does, the consequences. Will be severe. You don't need to be there for that."

"Please, Papà..."

He sighs, but finally nods. "Okay, figlio, take care of Schuyler first. We'll take care of Blaine after we know she's okay. Now go."

"Come on, Bastian. Gia said Schuyler's asking for you." My mam's pulling me towards the door.

I turn away from Blaine who has now passed out and is snoring. What a fucking asshole. The bleeding from his bullet wound seems to have slowed down... What a shame.

Chapter Seven

Sebastiano

When my mam and I get to the hospital, we see Gia pacing in the waiting room. Grady is trying to get her to sit down.

"Why are you out here? Where's Schuyler? Why aren't you with her?" I snap at her. She glares at me and I sigh. "Sorry, sis. Where's Schuyler?"

"They took her for an MRI and CT scan. They wouldn't let me go with her. I told them to do every test and make sure we know exactly what's wrong with her. Their initial check has shown a broken wrist, fractured tibia and a few broken ribs. It also looks like she has a concussion," she rambles to me.

I look at my sister and she understands exactly what I need to know.

"She wasn't raped," she whispers to me. I grab her and hug her tight.

Thank God for that. But I know that if Schuyler hadn't shot that asshole, I would have.

"Family of Schuyler Viñales."

I stand up with my mam, Gia and Grady. "We're Schuyler's family."

The doctor nods as he sees Gia. He eyeballs me and Grady. I think he's trying to decide if we did this to her.

"How is she? Can I see her?" I ask.

"She's getting settled into a room and the police have been called because of the extent of her injuries," he says.

I finally realize that he's looking at my clothes, and I remember that her blood is all over me.

"If you're implying I did this to her, no. I didn't fucking do this to her." I feel my mam's hand on my arm and I take a deep breath. We see Salvatore coming towards us with his partner. He looks pissed.

"I'm Officer Salvatore Mancini, you're Doctor McAdams?" Sal asks.

"I am, I've tried to talk to the patient and she won't give me any information. But it's obvious she was assaulted," he says while giving me side-eye.

"When can we see her?" Sal asks, ignoring the doctor's comments.

"As I told Mr...."

I guess he's not a hockey fan. Most people mistake me for Dom. "Mancini. Sebastiano Mancini." I try to keep my voice calm but all I want to do is put my hands around this doctor's neck and squeeze until he takes me to my woman.

He looks between Sal and me and frowns. A nurse comes up and lets the doctor know that Schuyler is settled and she's asking for Gia.

"I'll tell her you're here," Gia says to me. Grady follows them. Right now he won't let her out of his sight.

"I need to see her," I say to no one in particular. I watch them walk away with the nurse. I feel my mam put her arms around me, I take a deep breath. "I can't lose her, mam."

"I know, amore. You won't." She holds me and rubs my back like she did when I was a little boy. It's soothing and helps me to relax a little while we wait.

Giovanna

"When will we get her results?" I ask the nurse as we walk to Schuyler's room.

"Even though there weren't any signs of rape, we made sure to test for everything along with the MRI and CT scan," she says softly. "I requested a rush on the results. I'll bring them to you personally."

"Thank you so much." I take a deep breath and walk into Schuyler's room and breathe a sigh of relief when I see that she's alert. That's always a good sign.

"Is Sebastiano okay?" is the first thing she says to me. With everything she's been through tonight, her first concern is my brother.

"He's okay. He's here waiting to see you."

"But he can't see me like this." She starts sobbing. "This is my fault, I just didn't know how to leave him."

I go over and hold her. She's sobbing so hard that I can barely understand what she's saying. "Skye, he doesn't care what you look like. He just needs to be with you. And this is in no way your fault. Don't ever think you're to blame for Blaine's shitty choices." It makes me even angrier that he's made her feel like this is her fault.

She starts to calm down. I just sit with her and comfort her.

"Everything's going to be alright. Do you want me to call Mira?" I squeeze her hand.

"Yes please. She doesn't know anything about the abuse. I tried to keep it from her the best I could." She sniffles softly. "She's going to be so angry that I didn't tell her."

"It's going to be ok. I'll help you explain all of this to her. Do you want me to get Bastian for you while we wait for Mira?"

"A-are you sure he isn't mad at me?"

She sounds like a little girl worried that she's made the one person that matters mad at her. It's breaking my heart that we didn't do something sooner.

I hug her gently. "I promise. Bastian would never be mad at you for any of this."

She thinks for a bit and finally looks up at me and nods. "Okay. I'm ready to see him."

I kiss her head, then go back to my brother and mam. "She's ready to see you. She's scared that you're mad at her."

"I could never be mad at her. Why would she think that? Thank you, Gia," my brother says while the five of us walk back to Schuyler's room.

I can see the pain in his eyes and give him a hug. "Just show her she's loved. That's what she needs. Blaine beat her down more than any of us realized. It wasn't just the physical abuse, it was mental too. She's strong, but right now she's hurting."

I pull my phone out to call Mira, I was going to text her but this is too important.

"Hello?" Mira answers.

"Hey Mira, it's Gia Mancini. I'm sending my guard Grady over to pick you up."

"Why? What's going on? Is my sister okay?"

"Your sister is okay. But something happened and I would feel better talking to you in person."

"Okay. How long till he gets her?"

"He should be there in fifteen minutes. I'll see you soon."

"Thank you, Gia."

"You're both family, Mira. We'll always be here for you."

Thirty minutes later, Mira walks into the waiting room. I can see the panic in her eyes as she runs to me. I hold her tight, I can feel her trembling.

"A-are you sure Skye's okay?" she whispers.

"Yes. I promise, she's okay. She's hurt and it'll take time for her to heal. I wanted to sit and tell you what happened before you see her. Your sister loves you so much, you're the most important person to her. That's why she kept what was going on a secret from you."

Mira is staring at me while I start to explain.

"It was Blaine wasn't it? He did something to her? I used to hear them fighting sometimes. But whenever I would ask, she would tell me things were fine. I knew she was lying, but I didn't know how to make her talk to me."

I nod at her. "Blaine has been abusing Skye for the last year. Physically and mentally. He threatened to hurt you if she left so she stayed with him."

Mira drops to her knees and cries. "She left him six months ago. Then all of a sudden he was back. She told me she missed him and realized that she couldn't live without him. Fuck. She went back to him because of me."

"No, sweetheart. She did this *for* you. Not *because* of you. I would do the same for any of my family and that includes you and Skye." I wrap my arms around her. "The important thing to remember now is that she's rid of him. He'll never touch her again."

"I hope he dies a slow death and rots in hell for hurting my sister."

I nod. Me too, kid. Me too. I don't tell her I think that's exactly what's going to happen. She can find things like that out later.

"Are you ready to go and see her?"

"Yes."

"Keep in mind that he beat her pretty bad. But she's a fighter."

"Okay. Thank you so much, Gia. I'm so grateful that we have all of you in our lives."

I wipe the tears from my eyes and hug her one more time.

Sebastiano

I can't even explain the rage I feel when Gia tells me Schuyler thinks this is her fault. In no way is this her fault. I'm going to do everything I can to make sure she knows that. Even if it takes me the rest of my life.

"We'll wait out here. Let Skye know I need to at least get a quick statement from her tonight. I can get more details after she's rested," Sal says to me.

I hug him. "Thanks. I'm glad it's you that took the call."

I take a deep breath before I step into her room. Her eyes track me as I walk over and sit on the chair next to the bed. I take her hand and kiss it.

"Cuore mio," I whisper.

She starts bawling, and it's breaking my heart. I carefully get on the bed and hold her.

"It's going to be ok, Schuyler. You'll never have to deal with him again. I promise you that. No one will ever hurt you again."

"But I sh-shot him," she whimpers.

"Shh. Baby. Don't worry about that right now. Sal's outside and he needs to talk to you. Just tell him what Blaine did. I'll talk to him about the rest later."

"What? But I—I can't lie to Sal."

"You're not going to lie, baby. But you don't need to deal with all of it tonight. Sal needs to know that Blaine broke in and assaulted you. I promise I'll tell him the rest later."

She finally starts to calm down a little and nods.

"Everything's going to be okay. You don't have to hide anymore, you're safe now," I murmur in her ear. "I've got you."

I pull my phone out to text Sal, letting him know that he can come in. We hear a knock and I tell him to come in.

"Jesus, Skye," Sal says softly. "I'll make this as short as I can."

While Sal asks Schuyler questions, his partner is taking notes. When they're done, Sal comes over and gives her a kiss on the cheek.

"Don't worry about anything, Skye. That bastard is going to pay for doing this to you."

I carefully get off the bed and walk Sal out of the room.

He leans towards me. "I know there's more."

I look at him and nod. "They're at her house taking care of things." I don't have to say anything more, my cousin knows who and what I'm talking about.

"I'll text you when I get off."

We hug and I watch him head over to my sister and mam. I see that Mira is with them. After they say bye to him, they come into Schuyler's room.

"Cuore mio, this is my mam, Gráinne. Mam, this is my Schuyler."

My Mam smiles at Schuyler and comes over to kiss her head. "Welcome to the family, Schuyler."

We hear Schuyler sniffle at my mam's words. I get back on the bed with her, trying not to move her too much. She leans into me, my mam and Gia sit in the chairs around the bed.

She looks at Mira and bursts into fresh tears.

I look at my sister and my mam. They are the strongest women I know. After tonight, I know that they'll protect Schuyler like I will. I hold Schuyler until I know she's fallen asleep. I gingerly slide off the bed and gesture to Gia to come outside with me, leaving Mira and Mam sitting with Schuyler.

"I need you and Mam to stay with Schuyler."

She looks up at me. "Are you going to take care of Blaine?"

"I don't know. I just know that I need to be there. I need to know it's over. That he can never touch her again. And I need to find someone to be her Grady."

Gia sighs softly. "Okay, I'll stay. I need to call Declan. How much do you want him to know?"

"You don't have to lie or keep things from him, Gia. I trust him, he's part of the family."

She hugs me. "Thank you. It would kill me to have to lie to him."

"I know, Gia. I love you."

"I love you too."

I turn and leave before I can't. I hate leaving Schuyler right now, but I know she's in good hands.

And I need to take care of that bastard who put her in here.

I call my papà.

"*Is everything okay?*" he answers.

"*Sì, Papà. Where are you? I need to be there. Per favore.*"

I hear him sigh. But he gives me the address. I get into my car and drive. I'm imagining all the ways I want to end his life. But I know that I probably won't be allowed to do that.

When I pull into the warehouse lot, I see Sal pulling in at the same time. I get out and give him a hug before we both head inside. Blaine is sitting on the floor, my papà, zios and brothers surrounding him, along with Sal and Luca. There are four other men standing to the side—Elio Salvadori, Carlo Fenati, Mario Antonelli and Niccolò Marini. Elio is the Boss of the Southside Mafia and Niccolò is his consigliere. Carlo is his top capo and Mario his second capo.

I shake all their hands and then go over and hug my family.

"*Ti abbiamo aspettato.*" Elio says. *We waited for you.*

"Grazie." I nod at him.

"This *coglione* beat a woman? Your woman?" Mario asks in his thick Italian accent.

"Sì, this isn't the first time. He's been doing this for a while now," I answer him.

Mario kicks Blaine's leg. "You like hit women? Let us see how you are with someone your own size."

Luca snickers. Mario is bigger than all of us and can probably knock Blaine out with one punch.

"I just need a few minutes with him, then he's yours," I say as I take my shirt off and walk towards Blaine. Carlo hands me plastic protectors for my jeans and shoes. As I put them on, Blaine's eyes get wide.

"Y-you can't t-touch me," he stutters out. He tries to back away, but there's nowhere for him to go.

"Where the fuck you think you are going? This what happens when you put hands on a woman." Mario smirks at Blaine. "You lucky! We so nice, we took out the bullet and stitch you up!"

"S-she deserved it, that cheating bitch! She used me!" He looks over at Sal. "You're a cop! You can't just stand there and let this happen. Fucking pig! And I know you were fucking her!"

Sal snorts. "I'm not a cop right now. Right now I'm just a Mancini. Also, I never touched Schuyler. I have more respect for her than that."

The guys laugh at Blaine and I think he's starting to get an idea of what's going to happen to him tonight.

I grab him and yank him upright so he's standing, facing me. "You'll never touch Schuyler again. In fact, you'll never touch another woman again, ever."

"My father will bring all you fuckers down," he

snarls. "You'll all spend the rest of your lives in jail getting fucked by the very ones you put in there."

I spend the next fifteen minutes taking out my rage from what he did to Schuyler on him. My arms are starting to feel heavy when I feel someone pull me back.

"Enough, figlio. I won't let you finish this, you can't live with his blood on your hands," my papà says. I allow him to pull me away and take a few deep breaths to calm myself down.

"We've got it from here, brother," Elio says to my papà.

I look at Blaine lying on the ground. "I wish I had stopped him before he got to her tonight. I could've saved her."

"The point is, she's okay now and he won't touch her or anyone ever again," Luca says.

"Amen to that," Zio Leo replies.

I take the plastic off and throw it in the burning barrel. Then wipe the blood off me and get dressed. Then look over at Elio, Carlo, Mario and Niccolò. "Grazie."

"Niccolò is going to help you out. He'll be your woman's guard from now on," Elio says to me.

"Are you okay with this?" I turn to Niccolò.

"Sì. I'll protect her with my life. No one will touch her again," Niccolò responds.

I stare at Elio. "Grazie. I don't have enough words to express what this means to me."

"Our families have always helped each other out. This time is no different."

Everyone hugs and we walk to the cars, leaving the rest of the Southside mafia to finish dealing with Blaine. When they're done, they'll get in touch with us. Dom gets into my car with me and Niccolò after taking my keys.

"Back to the hospital?" he asks.

I shake my head no. "I need to go home and shower. I can't see her like this."

"Okay," he says, driving us home.

While I shower, Dom shows Niccolò around the house and property, pointing out Gia and Rella's homes too. They're waiting for me when I walk back into the living room.

"Grazie again, Niccolò."

"Nico. Niccolò sounds like I'm in trouble," he says.

Dom snorts.

He's going to fit in with us just fine.

Schuyler

After talking with Mira and explaining why I couldn't tell her what was going on with Blaine, I fall asleep. When I wake up, Sebastiano still isn't back. I look around and see his mam on one cot, Mira and Gia on the other. Gráinne sits up and stretches. I start to reach for the water cup, but she comes over and gets it for me. She welcomed me to their family tonight. Family. Is it really possible that I could be with Sebastiano?

"How are you feeling, amore?" she asks me quietly. She sits in the chair next to me and hands me the cup.

"I feel relieved, but still scared. I want to believe this is over, but Blaine will never let me go," my voice trembles.

Gráinne is nodding. "I understand. You're our family now Schuyler, you and Mira. You won't have to worry about Blaine anymore."

"You don't understand. He said he would hurt Mira if I tried to leave him." My tears are falling steadily as I look over at my baby sister. I've never admitted that to anyone, but I feel like I can finally trust someone to know the truth. "I can't let him hurt her."

"Shh. That's something you'll never have to worry about again. You're both safe."

The door swings open and Sebastiano walks in. He goes over to his mam and gives her a hug and kiss. Then comes over and gets onto the bed with me. The rest of his family comes in after him, along with one guy I don't recognize.

Sebastiano

"Cuore mio, Mira—this is my papà, Enea and my

uncles, Antonio and Leonardo. My aunt Rosaura. You know my brothers and cousins. And this is Niccolò, he's your bodyguard, Schuyler, and will be with you from now on," I say as each of them come over and kiss her and Mira on the head.

"Nico. I keep telling Sebastiano it's Nico. Unless you're mad at me, then you can call me Niccolò." He smiles at Schuyler and winks at Mira.

"How are you feeling?" my papà asks Schuyler. He takes my mam's hand and helps her up. Then he sits on the chair, pulling her onto his lap.

"I'm better now, thank you. It's nice to meet you, Nico," Schuyler says softly.

I smile at everyone. I realize how lucky I am to have grown up in the family I have. And now? Schuyler makes it complete.

Fiorella and Cillian come barging in with Marco, who's yawning as he walks in behind them. There's a nurse running after them saying they can't just come in.

"Why am I the last one to be told anything?" Rella's pouting and I can't help but chuckle. "And who the fuck are you?" she points at Nico.

"Fiorella Zoraida Mancini! Watch that mouth of yours," my aunt scolds her. Luca and Sal are behind my aunt, almost on the ground from trying to hold back their laughter. Tears are streaming down their faces.

———————————————

Schuyler

———————————————

I grab my side. "Don't make me laugh. It hurts."

Fiorella's eyes soften while she looks me over. "Are you okay?"

I nod. "I'm okay now."

"Someone will tell me what happened. But not now. Now it's about you. What do you need? More pillows? Blankets?" she's rambling and the others chuckle. "What? Did any of you think to ask her if she needed those things? I mean fine. She probably doesn't need it since Bastian's covering her. But still."

"Thank you, Rella." I chuckle. "I'm good. I wish I could go home."

"They're probably going to keep you for a few days. Maybe a week," Gia says and I sigh dramatically.

"Oh God. You're going to be a pain in the ass patient, aren't you?" Sal teases.

I stick my tongue out at Sal. "I'm an angel. I would never cause anyone any problems."

Someone snorts as I make this declaration. I think it was Nico...Rude.

Everyone laughs.I love this family already, they make me feel so at ease.

"She's definitely a horrible patient. But if you're the sick one? Watch out cause she's on you 24/7 and won't take no for an answer." Mira laughs. "You have a battle on your hands, Sebastiano."

I squint at Mira. "Traitor."

Sebastiano

"Well, we should let these two rest and get back home," my papà says to the rest of the family. "We'll all be staying at the Evanston house until things calm down a little. Mira, we would feel a lot better if you would agree to stay there with us. Or you can stay with Gia or Rella."

Mira nods at my papà. "Okay, Mr. Mancini. I will stay with any of you. Thank you," she says softly.

"You can stay with me and Declan. Rowan will love you." Gia smiles.

"We'll talk tomorrow," my papà says to me.

I nod. "Sí, Papà."

"Thank you so much for everything," Schuyler says to all of them. I don't think she knows exactly what she's thanking them for. But she will soon enough. My girl is strong and I know we'll get through whatever we have to. Because now that I know what it's like to have her in my arms? I'm never letting her go.

Nico makes himself as comfortable as he can on a cot that's way too small for him. He's also made sure his cot is between Schuyler's bed and the door.

Even though he knows that Blaine won't be bothering us, he grew up like we did. You never leave things to chance. Plus there's Conrad. If anything that Blaine was babbling about is true, we're going to have more problems. A lot more, and I'm not looking forward to that at all.

Chapter Eight

Schuyler

I've been out of the hospital for a week now and Sebastiano hasn't left my side except to go to work. I look like shit, but he makes it a point to tell me how beautiful I am every day.

Today is Cap's birthday. He and Mama have invited the whole Mancini clan over to their house for dinner. I'm so excited for them to finally get to know each other.

Everyone is meeting up at our place and following us to their house. They live about an hour and a half south of us.

I never know what to get Cap for his birthday. Mama is so much easier, she loves a lot of the same things I do. I settled on a gift certificate for a cigar shop because lately he's been into cigars. Kind of a nasty habit, but there are worse ones, I guess.

Mira has taken a liking to Nico. She thinks I don't notice her glancing at him and talking to him every chance she gets. I think he likes her too, but he's focused on protecting me right now.

I text Mira.

Schuyler: 5 min out

Mirabelle: I'm waiting outside already (laughing emoji)

I laugh at her text.

"She's waiting outside," I tell Sebastiano.

He chuckles and pulls into her dorm parking lot. I look in the mirror and see Nico smiling at Mira. He definitely likes my sister and I know he would be good for her.

"Hi everyone." Mira smiles as she gets in.

"Hi, Mouse. We still have to pick up dessert," I tell her.

We stop to get cupcakes and doughnuts. You can't go wrong with cupcakes and doughnuts. Plus, I know Enea and Gráinne have gotten the cake for tonight. I got to see it when they got to our house. It's a mini firetruck and it looks so life like. Cap's gonna love it. There's even little people on it that look like each of us, placed around and in the truck.

When we get to their house, Cap is in the backyard

starting the grill and Mama is inside getting the food ready.

Mira and I head inside with all the Mancini women to help Mama. Sebastiano and Nico head out back to join Cap with all the Mancini men.

"Hi, Mama," I say as I go over to give her a hug and a kiss.

"My girls." She smiles, hugging me then Mira. "How are you both doing?"

"Good. School is fun and living in the dorms has been okay," Mira says as she helps chop stuff up.

"And you? Is your recovery going okay?"

"Yes, Mama. I wish I could go back to work already." I chuckle. "This is Gráinne, Rosaura, Giovanna, Fiorella, and baby Rowan."

Mama Lynn hugs each of them. "Thank you so much for coming tonight."

"Thank you for inviting us." Gráinne smiles.

"That cake looks amazing! Thank you so much," Mama says.

"Rosaura made it," Gráinne says.

"Holy crap! Really? That's some serious talent!" Mama exclaims.

Rosaura is blushing. "Thank you. It's just a hobby. I've been making the kids' cakes since they were little."

"Do you sell any? I know people who would pay big money to have this kind of cake," Mama says.

"I suppose it would depend on what they want. I might be willing to do it if I can." She smiles.

My two families are blending seamlessly and it's the best feeling I've ever had. I watch Gráinne and Rosaura help Mama make the salad and side dishes for dinner. They're talking like they've been friends forever.

Sebastiano

Nico and I head to the backyard with the rest of my family.

"Hey, Cap. Happy birthday," I say as I hug him. "This is my papà Enea, my uncles Leonardo and Antonio. My brothers Dom and Enzo, my cousins Salvatore and Gianluca."

They all shake hands and wish Cap a happy birthday.

"You're having a great season," Cap says to Dom.

"Thank you. You're a Hawks fan?" He smiles.

"I am. Also a Panthers fan and I can't wait to see your upcoming season." He nods to Gianluca.

Gianluca grins. "Thank you, sir. I'm hoping I do better than last year."

"I'm sure it's gonna be a great season." Cap smiles.

He starts to put the meat on the grill.

"Let me do that, Cap. You sit and relax, today is your day," I say as I take the tongs from him.

He laughs and thanks me, then brings out his cigar collection and offers them to everyone.

Zio Antonio takes one. "Thank you."

Cap

"I wanted to thank you for taking care of Schuyler," I say. "She's gone through so much in her life and I'm so angry that I didn't see what Blaine was doing to her."

"Don't be so hard on yourself. Men like Blackwell are really good at hiding who they really are. And they're also good at controlling the women they're with. They break them, mentally and physically. I've seen too many men like that," Enea says to me.

"I don't know how to not be mad. She's my responsibility. She may not be my blood, but from the day I met her, she's been family. I don't have any biological children, but I have Schuyler and Mirabelle."

Enea is nodding at me. "I understand completely. If someone hurt my Gia like that I don't know what I would do. Shit, Rella too. But I can promise you that Blaine will never touch Schuyler ever again."

I'm not sure how he can promise that. But the look in his eyes is telling me that he's serious.

I was born and raised in Chicago and I've heard all the stories about the Mancini family. But I also know that they've done a lot of good for our city in the last few years. So, mafia or not, they have my support forever.

I'm glad that Lynn told me to invite all of them, it makes me feel better about Sebastiano. He's got a great support system in his family and I can see the love and respect they have for each other. This is true family.

Sebastiano

Watching my girl with her chosen parents is magical. I can see why she's so strong. Cap and Lynn show each other so much love. It's like watching my own parents.

I wrap my arms around Schuyler as we all sit around the fire pit.

"How about s'mores?" Mira says.

"Ohhh. Smmmorrres." Gianluca smiles.

"I'll get the ingredients," Lynn says, standing up.

"You sit, Mama. I'll get them," Mira says.

"I'll help." Nico stands up and follows Mira.

"I think Mira and Nico like each other," Schuyler whispers to me.

I think I may need to come out of my Schuyler bubble more often and interact with other people a little. Because I did not see that one coming. Nico and Mira, interesting. At least Mira would be in good hands, Nico would be a good man for her.

"Are you okay with that?" I whisper back to her.

She nods and smiles at me. "I can't think of anyone better to protect Mira than Nico."

I think about it and nod in agreement. I know Nico

would protect Mira like he protects Skye. And well, he's already family, so I guess it works.

Schuyler

"Okay, time to open presents!" Mira claps.

I laugh. Mira has always loved gift-opening time. She always makes sure we have at least one gift to open on special occasions.

She hands Cap his first gift.

"That's from the Mancinis." She smiles.

We watch him open it. It's a gift certificate to The Mancini Grill, located in The Legacy Hotel.

"There's no limit on it, you just give the card to the server at the end of your meal," Enea explains.

"Wow, thank you." Cap smiles.

"Okay, this is from Skye and Bastian."

Cap's smile gets even bigger as he opens a box with a beautiful humidor. It's etched with a firetruck, his Captain's insignia and badge. When he opens the box, he finds the gift certificate.

"Thank you, baby," he chokes out as tears glisten in his eyes. "It's beautiful."

"The box was all Bastian," I say. "The gift certificate was me."

"Well I love them both. Thank you so much."

"And this one is from Mama."

Cap opens a box to find a beautiful knitted scarf and matching hat.

"Thank you, my love." He gets up and kisses Lynn.

"That's beautiful," Gráinne says. "I've always wanted to learn how to knit."

"I'll teach you, if you and Rosaura teach me to cook some authentic Italian and Irish foods. Oh! And to bake," Lynn answers.

"That's a deal." Gráinne chuckles.

"And last but never least is my gift." Mira makes a big showing of giving it to Cap as we all laugh.

Cap opens an envelope that contains a homemade gift certificate. It says 'Good for three car washes'.

"I love it, baby. Thank you."

We spent a few more hours at Cap and Mama's house. Tonight was one of those nights that will live in my memory forever. It's the night my two families came together as one.

Chapter Nine

Schuyler

It's been almost a month since the night Blaine attacked me. After spending a week in the hospital, Sebastiano brought me to his house which he shares with Domenico instead of taking me back to mine. Nico has moved in with us too. Gia lives to the left of us and Rella to the right.

Since then, Sebastiano has been slowly moving my stuff into his house. He thinks I haven't noticed. I had told him I could go back to my place, but he wouldn't listen. I'll admit I'm relieved to not be at my house. I don't really know if I can go back there, even though eventually I'll have to. I mean, I can't stay here with him forever. Can I?

Sebastiano hasn't left my side since that night. He

won't talk about what happened to Blaine, and I haven't heard from Blaine since. I know who the Mancinis are. They're a mafia family, old school. I've read news articles about the feuds back in the old days—people going missing, gun running, drugs. But I know that they've been helping to clean Chicago up lately, and doing business on the right side of the law. I still can't help but wonder if they made Blaine disappear. Is he dead? I mean, I did shoot him...

I'm still on leave from work and it's driving me crazy. At my last appointment, my doctor said it'll be at least another two to three weeks before I can be cleared to go back to work. Cap and Mama come to visit every few days. Cap says he likes Bastian, that he's a good guy and he's happy I have him.

Mira knows everything now, and comes by as much as she can. She was mad at first that I didn't tell her about the abuse. I said I needed to protect her and I would do it again if it meant that she was safe.

Sebastiano and I haven't defined what we are to each other. He kisses me when he leaves the house and when he comes home. But he never pushes me to do more. I know he wants to and so do I...But I just don't feel ready yet.

Sebastiano

Having Schuyler here has been everything to me.

She didn't fight it when I told her she was coming home with me. She also didn't fight me about Nico. I think having him around makes her feel safer because she's seen Grady with Gia, and Marco with Rella. She's been hinting that she needs to figure out what to do with her apartment. I know she's noticed her stuff slowly appearing here. I almost have her whole apartment cleaned out. I've also talked to her landlord and he agreed to let her out of her lease whenever she wants. Until then, I've been making sure her bills are paid and she has nothing to worry about except recuperating.

I know she's wondering what happened to Blaine. I don't know how much to tell her. Part of me wants to tell her everything. I want her to know that she never has to worry about him again. But I'm afraid that she'll hate me for what we did. Then there's the other part that says if I don't tell her everything, she could hate me for keeping it from her.

I hear voices and look up from my computer. Conrad Blackwell comes barreling into my office without even knocking. I stand up to my full height. "You can't just barge into my office," I snap at him. Gloria, my secretary, is running in after him apologizing to me. I put my hand up. "It's okay, Gloria. I'll handle this. Why don't you take an early lunch."

She thanks me and turns to walk out, but not before she glares at Conrad. I have to hold back a laugh.

"What do you want?" I stay standing because I

know it's making Conrad uncomfortable. He's a small, pudgy man and I tower over him.

"Where's my son?" he spits out.

"Why would you come to me about that? Who's your son?" Playing stupid is the best thing for now.

"I know you know who Blaine is. He told me he met you and your brothers at that stupid ball. That you were all over his girlfriend, that slut Schuyler."

I take a deep breath and tell myself that I can't react to him. Must. Not. Punch. The small fat man. "I don't know what you're talking about."

He steps closer to me. "I know that bitch is staying with you. Don't play stupid with me. Just because your father is Enea Mancini doesn't mean you're better than me or my son."

Just as I'm about to tell him to get the fuck out of my office, my papà walks in. By the look on his face, he heard what Conrad said to me. I can't help puffing out my chest a little, knowing my papà always has my back.

"You need to leave now. You have no right to barge into an executive office," Papà says. He comes and stands next to me.

"Your son needs to tell me where my son, Blaine, is. I haven't heard from him in a month. I know he has something to do with this. His mother's worried, he's never stayed away this long." His tone noticeably changes now that he's talking to my papà. Asshole.

"I'm sorry your son is missing, Conrad. But I don't know why you think my Sebastiano would know where he is. They're not friends."

"I know that Blaine's girlfriend is staying with Sebastiano."

I'm getting pissed listening to Conrad talk to my papà like I'm not even in the fucking room. This is my damn office and he needs to get the fuck out.

"I don't know where you're getting your information, Conrad."

"Please don't talk to me like I'm an idiot, Enea. I know it's true and I don't really care because I never liked Schuyler anyway. She's beneath Blaine and I'm glad he finally got rid of her. I just want to know where my son is." His face is getting redder and puffier with every word.

I look over at my papà, waiting to see what he's going to say. I was about to say something but I saw the look on my papà's, face so I kept my mouth shut.

"Again, I'm sorry you haven't heard from Blaine. But I'm sure if Sebastiano knew anything, he would be the first to tell you. Now, you need to leave. And don't ever come in here without an appointment." My papà straightens to his full height of six-seven. I watch Conrad visibly shrink as he looks up at my papà.

"Then I have no other choice than to go to the police with this," he stutters out, his face turning an even brighter shade of red.

"You do whatever you feel you need to do, Conrad."

He turns and stomps out of my office and slams the door.

"Now I know why Blaine is such an asshole," I say

quietly to my papà. He nods at me as he stares at the door.

"That man is going to be a problem for us," my papà says.

"Papà? What should I tell Skye? She hasn't asked yet, but she has to be wondering why he just stopped coming after her." I make sure I'm keeping my voice low while we talk.

"That's something you'll have to figure out, figlio. How much do you want her to know? Can she handle the whole truth?"

I take a deep breath and think about it. "I think she can. She's started to open up to me about what she went through with him and why she stayed. She knows he could've killed her. She's going to be my wife and I won't have secrets from her." I get choked up thinking about that night. I could've lost her before I'd even had a chance to know her.

"Maybe we should have a family dinner, the whole family, and we can all be there when you talk to her. Then she'll know she'll never have to be alone again," my papà suggests.

"I think that would be good. She's never had any family besides Mira. Cap and his wife have tried, but I think she still keeps them at arm's length sometimes. But now with Blaine gone, she might be able to open up to everyone. When can we do this? Is tonight too soon?"

"Tonight's fine. I'll call everyone and let your mam

know." My papà hugs me. "It's going to be okay. She'll understand what happened and why."

"I hope so, Papà. I don't know what I'll do if she leaves me."

I watch my papà as he leaves my office. I take another deep breath and text Skye.

> Sebastiano: Cuore mio, how do you feel about having dinner with the family tonight?

> Schuyler: Sure. What time?

I let out a breath I didn't realize I was holding in.

> Sebastiano: Papà said seven. I'll be home in an hour. Just a few things to wrap up. How are you feeling?

> Schuyler: Okay. I'm BORED. I want to go back to work (crying emoji)

> Sebastiano: Soon, cuore mio, soon. Do you need anything before I come home?

> Schuyler: No, I don't need anything, thank you. See you soon. Please drive safe

> Sebastiano: Always, amore. See you soon

I haven't told her that I love her—I don't want to scare her off, especially after what she's just gone through, but it's time she knows. Today. No matter what happens after I tell her about Blaine, she'll know exactly how I feel about her.

I need to tell her what she means to me now, before we go to dinner. I haven't been shy about my feelings. I haven't pushed her for sex because I don't want her to think that's all I want from her. But holy fuck, I want her so damn bad. I stop at a flower shop to get her a bouquet of tulips. I remember her saying how much she loves them.

Perfect, Dom's car is gone when I get home.

"Honey, I'm home!" I call out. I hear Schuyler giggling and I follow the sound. This woman is everything, she makes my heart full. I find her in the kitchen with Nico. I walk up to her and hand her the tulips.

"I'm going to go get ready. Let me know when it's time to go." Nico chuckles.

I nod and wait for him to leave. Then I grab Schuyler and kiss her, she moans softly as she kisses me back.

I pin her against the counter and grind my cock against her body. She reaches down and pops the button on my pants...

"Are you sure, amore?" I whisper. "You know I'll wait forever for you."

She runs her hands down my chest. "I'm sure. I want you. I need you," she moans. "Please."

I pick her up and take her to our room, then gently lay her on the bed. She doesn't take her eyes off me as I slowly get undressed. I get down to my boxers, then work on her clothes. I want to just rip them the fuck off of her, but I restrain myself and take my time. I slowly undress her, paying extra attention to her perfect breasts. That gets a growl out of her and I chuckle as I keep moving down her body.

"You are so fucking beautiful," I whisper while she helps me slide her jeans off. I rub her clit then slowly slide a finger in her, keeping my eyes on her.

"Bastian," she gasps.

I add another finger and bring her to the brink of orgasm, then stop.

"Why the fuck would—" she starts to grumble.

I slide my body up hers and capture her lips as I slide into her slowly. I hold her hands above her head and start moving. If I'm not careful I'm going to embarrass myself. But fuck we fit together like we were made for each other. I feel her hands on my ass.

"Fuck me please," she moans.

"I will never say no to you," I growl and move faster. I feel her shatter around me, her walls clenching my cock until I can't hold back anymore. "Cuore mio." I push into her one last time and find my release. I wrap my arms around her and try to catch my breath.

I kiss her gently. "I love you, Schuyler. I'm never letting you go."

Schuyler

Holy shit. Sebastiano just said he loved me. I had lost hope of ever finding the one for me. He tightens his hold on me. I bury my face in his neck and breathe him in.

"You're everything I've always wanted," I say. "I don't want you to ever let me go."

His beautiful face breaks out into a smile. God I love his smile, it makes his whole face light up, and his eyes? His eyes are a swirl of blues and greens glittering at me.

"We should take a shower. Are we having dinner at your parents house?" I ask.

"Yeah, it's a pretty long drive, but you'll love our town. I can't wait to show you around."

I smile at him and get up. "Are you coming? Or are you going to just lie there?" I tease him. He jumps up, scoops me into his arms, and heads to the bathroom.

"Later on we'll use the jacuzzi." He smirks, turning the water on while keeping his hold on me.

An hour later we're heading out to his hometown. We're only thirty minutes behind...It was his own fault for looking so damn sexy.

Chapter Ten

Sebastiano

The drive to my hometown with Schuyler is different than driving it by myself. We took her car, it's a BMW M8 competition coupe. She loved Gia's car so much I surprised her with her own last week.

I'm nervous as hell for her to find out what happened to Blaine. I know she's happy to be rid of him, but it's different to be rid of him and to be rid of him. She's going to find out my family still has ties to the illegal side of the mafia world. We've worked hard at getting past that and trying to do things right, but our family has been a part of the mafia world since before my nonno and nonna came here to America. It's our history and a way of life that we'll always be part of.

I'll never regret what we did to Blaine. Not only did it save my girl from him, it saved other women from ever falling into his trap.

When we arrive in Lake Renegade Township, I drive around the town and point things out to her before heading to my parents home.

"I forgot how nice your town was," Nico says from the backseat.

"How long has it been since you've been here?"

I pull into the driveway and past the gates that lead to my parents' main property.

"It's been about fifteen years. I remember wishing our town had a lake too." He chuckles. "And I remember your house. It's changed since I last saw it. That garage is new, yes?"

"That building over there? Yeah, they built that about seven years ago. For the extra cars, bikes and toys." I laugh.

"You guys always had the best toys." Nico smiles.

"Holy crap, you grew up in that?" Schuyler gasps.

I chuckle. "Sì, cuore mio." I look over at her and her eyes are huge.

"Wow. It's extraordinary."

"Grazie. My grandfather Pietro, my father's father, built the original structure and over the years they just kept adding onto it."

"That's so awesome. I love that it has so much family history. Where do your uncles live?"

"One of the changes that my papà and uncles made

was to split the house into three sections. So they all live here too."

"Like a triplex? You all grew up together here?"

"We did. And well it's kind of like a triplex. The garages separate the sections. You have to go through them to get to each house. You'll be able to see what I mean when we get inside."

I park in front of the house and see that almost everyone's here already.

"Those are really big garages." She giggles.

"Helps with soundproofing." I chuckle. "Four car garages."

I run around the car and open the door to help her out, pulling her to me and kissing her. "I still can't believe how lucky I am to have you with me."

Schuyler

I blush listening to Sebastiano. "I'm the lucky one. I was at a point where I thought that was just my life. That I would have to live with the abuse forever. Then I met you, and you opened my eyes to what could be. Even after meeting you, I didn't think I would ever get away from Blaine. So I never truly let myself imagine how being with you could heal me and make me whole again."

"Cuore mio. You had me from the moment you said hello to me at the ball. I never thought being with someone could be like this. I can't imagine it would be like this with anyone else, only with you. I knew there wasn't anything I wouldn't do to make you mine."

I reach up and touch his face, then kiss him. I moan softly when I feel his hands on my ass.

"Okay you two, you're in public for fuck's sake." Enzo comes out of the house, making faces at us.

Sebastiano laughs, hugging Enzo who then hugs me and shakes Nico's hand.

"How can you stand being around these two?" Enzo asks Nico while still making faces.

"I'm good at tuning them out." He smirks. I smack his arm and he laughs more. Smacking Nico is like smacking a rock—with a face.

"Is everyone here?" Sebastiano asks Enzo.

"No. Dom, Declan and Cillian are on their way, practice ran late. Everyone else is here though," he responds.

Sebastiano takes my hand and the four of us head into the house.

"Oh my God. It smells heavenly in here," I say, taking a deep breath.

"Mam's the best cook. She usually makes Irish and Italian foods. Tonight smells like Irish stew and soda bread. And if I know Papà, he'll have requested tiramisu for dessert," Sebastiano says as he leads me further into the house.

Sebastiano

"Where's everyone?" I ask Enzo.

"Mam, Zia, Gia and Rella are in the kitchen. Last I saw, Mam was making an emergency lasagna. Papà and zios are out checking the campgrounds because the perimeter alarms went off earlier. The rest of us were watching TV. I heard you pull up, so I came in to be nosy."

I snort. "You're a dork. You think they need help at the campgrounds? I wanted to show them to Schuyler anyway."

He shrugs his shoulders. Yeah, brothers are a lot of help. I roll my eyes at him and right when I'm pulling my phone out to text my papà, Gia comes out of the kitchen.

"See! I told you they were here!" she yells back towards the kitchen. I hear all of the women laughing. She gives both of us a hug. "I told them I heard your car and they didn't believe me," she says, making faces as she hugs Nico too.

I laugh at her. Schuyler starts to follow Gia into the kitchen.

"Where are you going, amore?"

"All the women are in the kitchen."

I smile and kiss her. "You can join them when we come back."

"Come back? Where are we going?"

"I want to show you the campgrounds. I just need to text Papà first."

"Are you sure? I don't want your mam to think I'm lazy and don't want to help."

Gia chuckles. "Don't worry, Schuyler, go see the campgrounds and I'll let Mam know where you went. Besides, she doesn't really need help, we're just there to keep her company while she cooks."

"Really? I feel bad that I'm the only one not in there."

Gia hugs her.

"It's okay, we'll be back soon," I say.

> Sebastiano: Papà do you need help at the campgrounds? Schuyler and I just got here and I wanted to show her around

>> Enea: We're okay here. But if you want to bring her, you can. Just had a minor misunderstanding with a camper about boundary lines

> Sebastiano: Okay, we'll head over there now. See you in a few

>> Enea: Okay figlio

"I'm going to take Schuyler over to the campgrounds," I say to Gia and Enzo.

"I'll come too," Enzo says while grabbing his jacket. "We can take the side-by-side."

"What's a side-by-side?" Schuyler asks.

"Ooh. You've never been on a side-by-side?" Enzo chuckles. "You're gonna love it. I'm driving!"

"Hey! I'm older, I should drive!" I grab Schuyler's

hand and drag her with me, chasing Enzo out to the garage where we keep the four-wheelers. He's already sitting in the driver's seat. What a dick—and he's grinning at us like a madman.

"Get in!" He claps like a little kid. Nico's sitting in the passenger seat, looking a little worried about Enzo driving.

I roll my eyes at him and help Schuyler get in. She's giggling at Enzo and me.

"Fine. Onward, Jeeves! Vai!" I make a gesture like I'm cracking a whip at him, complete with sound effects.

He stomps on the gas. "Hold on!"

"You're crazy!" Schuyler shouts while laughing and holding onto the bar in front of us. Nico looks like he's going to throw up. He's holding onto the bar in front of him for dear life.

I love seeing Schuyler so happy and carefree. She was so different when we first met. Always looking around for Blaine, making sure she wasn't caught doing something that would set him off. Now she's like a whole new person and I love it.

We drive into the campgrounds, heading to the main area to meet up with our papà and uncles. When we get to the main office, I help Schuyler get out of the side-by-side. I pull her to me and kiss her.

"It's beautiful here." She smiles.

"We own a little over five hundred acres. This part of the preserve is for campers. You see the fence that separates our area from the campgrounds. There's cameras and motion detectors that alert us if anyone tries to hop over the fence or go into areas that are restricted. Once they get too close, the lights and cameras kick on. If they jump over the fence, sirens blare and we can talk to them through the intercom to let them know they're trespassing. The campers usually listen, but we come over and check no matter what. Before we all moved out, we were the ones to help check the campgrounds. But now, my mam's guard, Arturo, comes out with my papà and zios when they need to check the grounds. There are about ten cabins, all different sizes, that people can rent. They can also camp in tents or RVs. We have the hookups for the RVs over there."

"Can we camp here? I think it would be nice to lay out by the lake and watch the stars."

"Of course. But you haven't seen the lake that surrounds my parents house. You may like that one even more. It's smaller, but it's where we used to camp and stuff when we were growing up."

"That sounds wonderful. Your parents won't mind?"

"Cuore mio, my parents love you more than they love me. They'll never say no to you." I chuckle.

"Your parents are really great. Thank you for sharing them with me." She hugs me.

I wrap my arms around her. "I told you, you're mine. And that makes you part of my family. Every person here will have your back no matter what."

I feel her sigh and hold me tighter.

My papà and zios come over and give us a hug.

"This is all so beautiful," Schuyler says to them.

"Grazie. You should have Bastian take you to the lake. The sun will be setting soon and it's a spectacular sight to watch it set over our lake," Zio Tonio says.

I chuckle. My Zio Antonio is the original ladies man. He's never been married and has no children. Everyone used to make bets on how long he would be a bachelor. No one has won yet because here he is, still single and no kids—that we know of. I still think one day he'll meet The One. I believe everyone has one, especially now that I've met Schuyler.

"Are you okay, Nico?" my Zio Leo asks.

"Enzo should never be allowed behind the wheel of anything with a motor," Nico answers. He still looks a bit pale.

"Hey! I'm a great driver!" Enzo defends himself. "It's not my fault you have a delicate stomach."

"Why do you think I tried to get to the side-by-side first?" I laugh at Nico.

"You could've warned me." He frowns, which makes me laugh even more. Schuyler snorts, which gets her a dirty look from him too.

"We all know not to get in with Enzo." Zio Leo laughs.

"Why did no one tell me? My fucking life flashed before my eyes more than once—and the ride was only ten minutes." He's whining and it's hilarious.

"The ride was only five minutes. And I'm an

excellent driver," he says again, making all of us laugh even harder.

"No Enzo. Your family loves you so they won't tell you. But I will. You suck at driving." Nico mocks Enzo.

"Well if I'm that bad at driving, you can walk back to the house." He smiles smugly.

Chapter Eleven

Schuyler

I had the most wonderful time with Sebastiano's family tonight. Growing up, Mira and I only had one foster family that liked to have dinner together. But sadly, we were only with them for a few months before we were moved to another home. It was the only foster home that felt like a real home and tonight's dinner reminded me of that time.

"Thank you for this delicious dinner," I say to Gráinne.

"You're welcome, amore," she replies, smiling as she leans on Enea.

"I wish I could cook like you do. When I got custody of Mira, we lived on microwave dinners and ramen. I mean I can cook a few things but nothing like this." I chuckle watching Sebastiano's parents. They're the perfect picture of true love, the way they look at each other is everything. Whenever I look at them, they're touching each other. Whether they're holding hands or just touching fingers.

"I would be happy to teach you anything you want. I've been teaching Gia and Rella all my secrets, you can join us anytime."

"That would be fun! I would love to learn how to cook like you." This family is incredible. It's taking all I have to keep from bursting into tears. But I wonder why she said she's only started teaching Gia now? Wouldn't this be something Gia would've grown up learning?

Sebastiano takes my hand.

I look over at him and see some conflict in his beautiful eyes. Is this when he decides to leave me? My hands start shaking, he grasps both of them and kisses me.

"I have some things I need to tell you. And I wanted my family to be here when I tell you because you're part of this family now." He's looking into my eyes.

I nod slowly, but my stomach is still in knots.

"I want you to know how much you mean to me. That night we met at the ball, the life I thought I wanted changed. I knew in that moment that I found my one. My person, the one who made my soul complete. I love you. I love everything about you."

This is the second time Sebastiano has said he loves

me. And this time in front of his entire family. Do I love him? Of course I do. I knew the night of the ball that he was the one I wanted. But because of Blaine, I never thought I could be with him. Yet here I am, sitting with the family I've always dreamed of, for me and for Mira. A mom and dad who truly love their children, and siblings that would do anything for each other. Then there's the uncles, aunt and cousins. I open my mouth to say that I love him too when I hear Enea clear his throat.

"Schuyler, we love having you and Mira in our family. You both bring so much to us as a clan. But there are things you need to know. We protect each other no matter what and because of that, you and Mira will never have to worry about anything ever again."

Sebastiano holds me closer while we listen to his papà.

"As head of the family, I feel that you need to know what happened the night Blaine attacked you. I know you've probably been wondering where he's been. I won't go into details, all you need to know is that he'll never bother you again. And if anyone ever hurts you or Mira, you come to us and we'll always protect you."

"D-do you mean Blaine is dead?" I blurt out.

"Sì, amore. He is gone, are you okay with that?" Enea confirms what I've been thinking these last few weeks.

"I need to know what happened. Please," I beg Enea. He looks at Sebastiano and the others before taking a breath and sighing.

"Are you sure you really want to know?" he asks.

I let out the breath I was holding in. "Yes. I'm sure. I lived with his abuse for over a year. I never thought I would get away from him. And now that he's gone...I need to know what happened. I remember shooting him and I thought he was going to die from that. But from the way you're talking, I don't think he did."

"No, he didn't die from the gunshot wound," Enea starts off. He explains that Blaine was taken to another location where he was shown what it felt like to be me. All the injuries he gave me, he was given.

I take a minute to let it sink in. He didn't die from the gunshot. But he is dead because of what he did to me.

When Enea's done explaining, I can't say that I'm sad. I don't know if that makes me a horrible person or not. The Mancinis did this for me. They did it to end the abuse.

Salvatore clears his throat. "There's something everyone needs to know. Conrad Blackwell filed a missing persons report for Blaine. He told my captain that he suspects Sebastiano had something to do with his disappearance. So my captain called me into his office today and asked me if I knew anything. I told him all I know is that Schuyler's staying with Sebastiano and Domenico because of a break-in at her home."

"Grazie for the heads up," Papà says. "The only ones who know are us and the Southside Mafia. I don't doubt their loyalty to us, like they'll never doubt ours to them. So we have nothing to worry about there. We need to make sure none of us let Conrad get under our skin. No matter what he says to any of us or about us, we can't react to him."

Then he looks over at me and asks, "Are you okay?"

I nod slowly at Enea. "I can't believe you all did this for me. I mean because of what Blaine did to me. And now you may have huge consequences. I don't want anything to happen to any of you because of me."

"Amore, none of us would change anything that we did for you." Gráinne looks me dead in the eye. "Don't ever feel like we regret any of it. And none of it was your fault, don't you ever blame yourself for what you went through or for what happened to him. He doesn't deserve any of your sadness or pity. No real man would ever touch a woman like he touched you."

My eyes fill with tears and I wipe them away as I look at each of the Mancinis sitting around the dining table.

They're all looking steadily back at me. In the past I would be worried about seeing pity from people, but tonight? All I see is love coming from each and every one of them. I don't know how I got so damn lucky. "Thank you."

I feel lighter knowing that Blaine will never be able to hurt me or anyone ever again.

Spending time with the Mancini family is everything to me. I'm so grateful that Mira has adapted so well. I don't know what I would do if they didn't get along. Watching all of them laugh and joke around with each other warms my heart.

They're a big family, but they never seem to leave anyone out. Everyone's always included in the conversations, even Rowan. He's such a good baby. I've been watching Sebastiano with him for the last thirty minutes. Watching him be an uncle to Rowan makes me want that future with him. Babies, marriage, forever. I just hope that's what he sees for us too.

I blush when I see Sebastiano staring back at me. I smile at him and he winks at me while Rowan is babbling at him. He's talking to Rowan like he's having a real conversation. It's the cutest thing I've ever seen.

Driving home, I can't stop smiling. I'm free. I'll never have to look over my shoulder again. And I can give all of myself to Sebastiano.

Sebastiano

I turn my alarm off, roll over and wrap my arms around Schuyler. She's gone back to work and she's so much happier. Nico goes with her to the station for every shift. Schuyler finally told Cap and Lynn the whole story the night of his birthday. After hearing all of it, Cap agreed to having Nico at the station. He was pissed that she never told him, but she explained how he was threatening Mira. That she didn't know how to get away from him and still keep her safe. She also told him that I rescued her and made her whole again.

His answer to all of that? Blaine better not show his face around him ever again.

I wanted to say that won't be a problem.

I love going to see her at the firehouse. I've gotten to know Cap and his wife, and I'm really glad that she's had them this whole time. And Mira? She's a great kid, Schuyler's done such an awesome job raising her. I can't help but imagine our children—they're going to have the best mother.

I've been trying to figure out when to propose to Schuyler. I have the ring. I've had it since she came home from the hospital. I don't want to rush her, but I also don't want to wait.

I try not to bother her too much at work, but let's face it—I can't stand being away from her and the drive to see her from my office isn't that bad. Plus I'm my own boss, so I just take long lunches every third day.

We've been trying to be proactive about the situation with Conrad Blackwell. We have a restraining order barring him from stepping foot on any Mancini-owned property. The order also says that he needs to stay away from Schuyler and Mira. That includes the firehouse and Mira's school.

Conrad has also been voted off the board of Mancini Legacy Enterprises. The other members didn't like that he was pointing the finger at me for Blaine's disappearance. Especially after hearing about what Blaine did to Schuyler.

Sal keeps us in the loop when it comes to what's going on in his department. The police are saying that

Blaine probably went off on a bender and will come back when he's ready. They're not actively looking for him because he's gone missing before.

Conrad has threatened to go to the press if they don't start looking for him. If he does that, then Sal's captain will have no other choice than to officially open an investigation.

Chapter Twelve

Sebastiano

I originally planned a sexy getaway for Schuyler and me. But then I realized that I'd have to bring Nico. Then Dom heard about it. After that it was like a domino effect and before I knew it, all of my siblings and cousins were going. So now it's a family vacation. Somehow we've been able to keep it from Schuyler.

We will be in Hawaii for eight days. We're spending the first half of our vacation on Maui and the last half on Oahu. I'm so excited, my family used to go to Hawaii every year. We own homes on Maui and Oahu and that's where we'll be staying.

Our home on Maui is in Ka'anapali and our home on Oahu is on the North Shore, where the famous surf tournaments are held. I'm hoping that the Eddie Aikau

Big Wave Invitational will be going on while we're there. It's a special tournament that's only held when the waves are consistently twenty feet high. And the surfers have to be invited to participate, hence the name. Schuyler is going to love it.

She's on shift today and I'm trying to pack a bag for each of us. I choose things I love to see her in. I know that's probably not fair, but if she needs anything else, we can just buy it there.

> Sebastiano: Hungry? Should I bring pizza?

> Schuyler: Sure. We were just arguing about who's turn it was to cook. LOL

> Sebastiano: LOL. Who's turn is it?

> Schuyler: I think it's Rhys' turn but he's a lazy ass

> Sebastiano: Well I'll be there in about 40 min. Love you

> Schuyler: Okay baby, thank you. Love you too

I smile and grab my shit to leave.

"Where are you going?" Dom asks.

"Taking Skye and the guys some pizza. Want me to bring some home?"

"Yes, please."

I laugh and head out.

When I get to the firehouse, I walk inside and find the three of them watching TV.

"Nice to see you're all so busy," I tease, setting the pizzas down.

I go over and give Schuyler a kiss and fist bump Cap, Rhys and Nico.

"Thanks for dinner." Cap smiles. "You're saving Rhys' ass."

"Psh. It's not my turn. It's Skye's turn," Rhys says as he shoves a piece of pizza into his mouth.

"See? This is what I deal with at work. So when you ask me how my day went, imagine this right here." Schuyler laughs.

I sit down and pull her onto my lap. "I love that you have a good time at work."

"It's never dull, that's for sure." She snickers.

Schuyler

I've gotten so spoiled having Sebastiano come and visit me at the station. Sometimes he brings food, but most of the time he just comes to say hi.

Dinner with his family last week was eye-opening. I had heard of the mafia ties the Mancinis have. But to hear it from them is a whole different story. I can't say it makes me feel any different about them, though. I love them for what they've done for me and if anything, it makes me feel even more special now that they've taken Mira and me into their family.

We've had Cap and Mama for a while now, and now we have the Mancinis. That's more family than I ever thought we would have.

Just as we're finishing eating, the alarms sound and the announcement for a residential fire comes on.

"Be safe, cuore mio," Sebastiano says.

"Always." I smile.

Sebastiano

Since our flight is at seven in the morning, I double check to make sure everything is ready to go, so that we can leave as soon as she gets home. It's going to be hard to sleep, but I need to, otherwise I'll be useless our first day in Hawaii. It's going to be a great trip, just me and my girl...and the family.

My alarm wakes me up at four. Getting up this early is bullshit and people shouldn't have to do it. Oh wait, today is the perfect day to get up at four. HAWAII.

I text Nico.

Sebastiano: Any delays?

Niccolò: Nope, leaving in a few

Sebastiano: Okay, you need time to pack?

Niccolò: No, I packed last night

Sebastiano: Good boy, Nico

Niccolò: Bite me. Or I'll just tell Skye what's going on

Sebastiano: You wouldn't

Niccolò: Try me

Sebastiano: Dick

Niccolò: I learned from you. Now shut up, Skye is ready to leave

I snort. Then I open the group chat with everyone.

Sebastiano: Everyone ready? Are we carpooling?

Gianluca: Heading to your place now, just picked up Mouse. We should be there in about 15 min

Declan: Gia's getting Rowan's things together for your parents. We're ready when you are

Fiorella: (yawning emoji) Ugh. Too early. Next time can we take a later flight? I mean we own the freaking plane

Sebastiano: (eye rolling emoji)

My parents are staying at Declan and Gia's house to take care of baby Rowan and their dog Atlas. I know my sister is having a hard time leaving the baby. But she and Declan need to have time together too. Eight days is a lot, and if it gets to be too much, Gia said they would just come home sooner.

Everyone begins to show up, it should take another fifteen minutes or so for Schuyler and Nico to get here. I don't remember the last time I was so excited about a vacation. I can't wait to see Schuyler's face when she realizes where we're going.

Schuyler

Nico is being unusually quiet on our drive home. He's usually the one chattering away.

"What's wrong with you?" I ask him.

"What do you mean?"

"You're really quiet. Normally you talk a lot."

"Are you saying I'm noisy?"

"Um. No?"

He rolls his eyes at me and I snicker. As we get to the house, I see Sal's car. I wonder what he's doing here this early?

"Is there something going on today that I don't know about?"

"Huh?"

Nico doesn't do innocent well. Now I know

something's up. It's not my birthday, or anyone's, for that matter. At least I don't think so.

Walking into the house, I hear a lot of voices. Seems like everyone is here this morning. I feel my anxiety level creeping up and start to wonder if something bad happened. Then I see suitcases lining the foyer wall. Someone's moving in? Or out? It's only Sebastiano, Dom and me, so...

"Cuore mio." I turn and see my love walking towards me with a huge smile on his face.

"Is someone moving in?"

"No." He laughs. "I have a surprise for you. Did you want to grab a quick shower? We have to leave in thirty minutes and you won't be able to shower till tonight."

Huh. I sniff at myself. "I think I should, I smell like the station."

I hear Sebastiano and Nico laughing as I walk upstairs to shower. I want him to follow me, but I know that if he does there's no way we're leaving in thirty minutes.

Sebastiano

Watching Schuyler walk away is hard. Really *hard*. Dammit. I need to walk away, preferably not towards my family. Kitchen. That's a good idea.

"Anyone want a drink?" I call out as I head to the

kitchen.

I hear a few of them say yes and I grab some bottles of water.

"Are we calling for a car?" Gia asks as she passes the water out.

"Yeah, that will be better than leaving ours at the airstrip," Sal answers her as he gets on the phone.

Schuyler comes down fifteen minutes later. I grab her and kiss her. "Beautiful."

She smiles up at me and says thank you.

"Where are we going?" She asks.

"It's a surprise."

"Ugh. Not even a hint?" She asks the others for help.

"Sorry." Luca snickers.

"Yeah, you sound sorry." She sticks her tongue out at him.

Schuyler

They're all acting weird. I glare at each of the Mancinis and their other halves, squinting my eyes the hardest at Mira. My baby sister, my partner in crime. Traitor. And Nico, can't forget him.

Marco snickers so I glare at him too.

"Okay, time to go!" Fiorella exclaims and everyone scrambles.

The guys grab the bags, and Gia, Rella and Mira

grab me to pull me towards the car. If no one is going to tell me what's going on, I'm not gonna make it easy for them. So I drag my feet.

Sebastiano comes up behind us and picks me up. Shit. He kisses me, laughing as he deposits me into the waiting car.

I continue to pout because why not?

"Aww. Come on Skye, you love surprises," Gia says.

"She loves surprises, but she hates being the only one who's not in the loop," Mira teases.

Yeah, she's dead to me now. No more baby sister. No more Mouse. Buh-bye.

Great, now they're all staring at me.

We're parking at the Evanston Airstrip. Okay, clue number one is an airplane. I feel like my eyes are bugging out, I've never been on an airplane before.

I keep quiet cause I know no one is going to tell me where we're going. We board the plane and I see Sal go to the cockpit and talk to the pilot. Well shit, I guess they won't be announcing our flight plan.

Sighing, I kiss Sebastiano's cheek and then snuggle into his side.

"Thank you," I whisper.

"You don't even know where we're going."

"Just being on a plane is an adventure for me."

"You're welcome, cuore mio. Now rest, the flight is a long one."

He reclines our seats so they're almost laying flat. I close my eyes and fall asleep.

Sebastiano is waking me up and telling me to look out the window. I sit up and see the most gorgeous sight. Something I never thought I'd ever see in person. I tear up and look at Sebastiano.

"Are you for real? What did I do to deserve you?" I whisper as the tears stream down my face.

"You told me that your dream place is Hawaii. I want to make all of your dreams come true."

This man is everything. After growing up in foster care and then going through the abuse with Blaine, I never thought I deserved to be happy. I thought my only purpose was to take care of Mira and make sure she had the best life. But Sebastiano has shown me I am worthy of that same life—and love. I can decide what happens in my life and make it better.

"This is Captain Kawika. We'll be landing at the Kapalua Airport on the island of Maui in about ten minutes. The temperature is eighty-five degrees with clear skies. I hope you all enjoy your vacation here."

As we descend, my eyes are glued to the blue-green waters that remind me of my love's eyes. It seems to go on forever and I feel myself getting lost in the view. We get off the plane and I take a deep breath. It even smells different here. Salty and tropical, I love it so much. Maybe we can come back here if we get married.

I can't stop smiling. We get into the limo that's waiting for us.

"So you like your surprise?" My former Mouse asks.

I stick my tongue out at her and she laughs.

It's only about a ten to fifteen-minute drive to the Mancini estate. After Sebastiano shows me our room, we head straight outside and to the private beach. I step into the Pacific Ocean for the first time in my life.

"This is incredible." I breathe in deeply and smell the salt in the air. "Thank you so much," I say to everyone, who have all come with us down to the beach.

"You deserve everything," Mira says as she embraces me. "Thank you for always taking care of me. I don't know where I would be without you."

I hug her tight. "You are worth every mountain I had to climb to make sure you were okay. And I approve of you and Nico." The last part I whispered for just her to hear.

She looks at me, "How did you know?"

"I know everything about you, Mouse. There's nothing you can hide from me."

Mira smiles shyly and goes over to Nico. I watch him smile and wrap his arms around her. Everyone watches, some are shocked and the rest look like they knew all along too. This vacation is starting off in the best way.

"Should we all meet up for dinner?" Dom asks everyone.

"Sounds good. Why don't we meet back here at five. I'll make sure Leilani's is ready for us," Luca says.

We all go our separate ways, with some of the single guys hanging out together.

"What would you like to do, cuore mio?"

"I don't know, what is there to do here?"

"We could go to Lahaina town and walk around. Or we could stay here and hang on the beach."

"Hmm. Let's go and walk around." I smile.

Lahaina town was quaint and perfect. We walked around for a few hours and then headed back to the house to get ready for dinner.

The food at dinner was divine. Maybe it's because I'm eating in Hawaii, but it was the most delicious meal I've ever had.

The four days we were on Maui seemed to fly by. We went on a drive to Hana and had lunch at the cutest bistro. We also went to a place called Seven Sacred Pools, it was like being in Heaven. Iao Valley was lush and green and we dipped our feet in the cold-ass river. I also got to see my first black sand beach.

Now we're on our way to Oahu for our last four days in Hawaii. I'm a little sad that it's going so fast. But Sebastiano promised that we will definitely come back.

Oahu is just as much fun as Maui, but in a different way. It's a lot busier and metro-like. But the beaches are gorgeous. We were lucky enough to be there for the Eddie Aikau Big Wave Invitational. That is something I will never forget. The waves were enormous and watching the surfers was awe-inspiring. Men and women riding almost thirty-foot waves—the surf was so loud it sounded like being in a thunderstorm. We also got to see the Pipeline Masters, those waves were so impressive. I learned that the reason the waves curl the way they do is because of the reef. Surfers have my utmost respect.

Sebastiano

We have come to Hawaii once a year since I was a child. Being able to experience all of it through Schuyler's eyes is incredible. Everything is exciting to her, down to finding a shell in the sand. She's heard the stories from the locals about not taking lava rocks off the island. I told her again, just in case. We'll only take things we've bought for friends. You can never be too safe.

I loved that we got to see the Eddie Aikau Big Wave Invitational and the Pipeline Masters. I forgot how much I loved the waters in Hawaii and watching the professional surfers compete. Growing up, we all learned to surf when we visited. But I wish I could surf even a fraction as good as them.

I promised Schuyler that we would come back to Hawaii soon. My plan is to get married here. Now to find the perfect time to propose...

Chapter Thirteen

Schuyler

It's been three months since that night with Blaine. Three months of being with Sebastiano and I don't want anything to change. But there's this nagging feeling, like everything is going to come to a screeching halt and I'm going to lose it all.

I turn my head so I can watch Sebastiano sleep. He's the most beautiful man I've ever seen and my heart hurts thinking that there's any chance that I could lose him. He's the part of my soul that I was missing. The part that I'd lost hope of ever finding.

"Why are you staring at me?" he mumbles, keeping his eyes closed.

"I'm not staring at you." I giggle softly and touch his cheek. "I'm admiring you."

Sebastiano

I grab her. She squeaks and I start laughing.

"You're so damn beautiful," I murmur into her neck. "How did I get so fucking lucky?"

"I'm the one who's lucky. You rode in on your white horse and rescued me from the evil wizard."

I laugh out loud. "Evil wizard huh?"

She laughs with me and nods. "Except you're my mafia prince, not my wizard prince."

I can't believe that even after everything she's gone through this last year, she's been able to get past it and become this radiant angel. Cuore mio. Her ring is burning a hole in my pocket. It's a princess-cut diamond surrounded by my birthstone and Mira's. I'm just trying to find the perfect moment. I want it to be something she'll never forget because this proposal will be the only one she'll ever have.

"Dom has a game tonight and my parents are driving into town so we can all go together."

She's snuggling with me and nods. "I love game days. It sucks when I'm on shift and have to watch it on TV. Cap's always yelling at it and throwing stuff when they don't score."

I snicker. "We should invite him and Lynn. We have extra seats. Or we can do a suite if that's easier."

"I like sitting in the stands. I mean don't get me wrong, being pampered in the suite is nice too. But it's so much better watching it from the seats surrounded by all the screaming fans. And it's fun to watch them stare at you." She giggles.

I poke her in the side and laugh. "It's not funny. It's a pain in the ass. I told Dom he needs to dye his hair and wear different-colored contacts."

She laughs even harder. "Why does Dom have to do that? You could dye your hair or wear colored contacts."

I stare at her. "Me? Dye my hair? Wait. Are you saying you don't like my hair? And my eyes?"

Schuyler

I'm laughing so hard I can barely breathe. I'm trying to suck in air but I lose it again. The look of horror on Sebastiano's face is priceless. At this point, I'm gasping and snorting at the same time. It's not attractive, but I can't help it.

"I love your hair, baby." I finally get out. He's squinting his eyes at me and that makes me laugh all over again. "And your eyes, I get lost in them every time I look at you."

"Then why should I be the one to change it? Besides, it's Dom's fault. He's the one who decided to become a famous hockey player." He rolls his eyes at me.

"How come you and Enzo don't play hockey too?"

"I played all through high school with Dom. But I didn't have the drive and passion that he had to really make it. And Enzo...well, Enzo and Gia didn't grow up with us."

I cock my head to the side and look at him. I still don't understand why they didn't grow up together. "Can I ask why?"

He takes a deep breath. "When Dom and I were three, Enzo and Gia were kidnapped. At the time we didn't know who took them. Just that they were gone, and we were made to believe that they were dead. As Dom and I got older, our papà started to tell us about the feud with the Springfield Mafia. Their capo is Dorian Laurent. When we found the twins, that's when we learned who had taken them. My papà had his suspicions, but without proof, he couldn't risk escalating the war. At that time, Papà was transitioning into the role of capo for our town. My Nonno Pietro was ready to step down and enjoy being a nonno to all of us. Papà was a great boss from the start and no matter how much he was hurting, he would never attack someone without solid proof." He has tears pooling in his eyes as he's telling me this story. "And he didn't have the proof he needed to go after the Springfield Clan."

I never take my eyes off him while he's explaining everything. "When did you find them? Did they know they had been taken?"

"We found them a year ago, they had no idea that they weren't part of the Laurent family. Gia asked our papà not to harm Dorian or his sons and that's why there's been no retaliation for the kidnapping. I know that she and Enzo still talk to the Laurent boys weekly and see them as much as they can. I hate it, but I'm trying to be understanding. The brothers were just babies themselves when Enzo and Gia were taken. It's not fair though, we missed out on everything with them. And those fucking Laurents? They got to be there for everything."

I feel his tears falling on my arm. I want to kill this Dorian for what he's done to my new family. Who the fuck takes babies? And then to let them think they were dead? There's a special place in hell for people like that. The pain on Sebastiano's face is killing me.

"Do Gia and Enzo still talk to Dorian too?"

He shakes his head. "Not that I know of. The last time they talked to or saw Dorian was the day we all went to meet with him. Gia and Enzo needed closure. Gia's anger, fear and hurt was killing her relationship with Declan."

"I can't even imagine what any of you went through all those years. Did you ever think that they could be alive? Even after you were told they were dead?"

"My parents never stopped hoping. At the beginning, my mam didn't talk to any of us. She tried to be there for Dom and me, but most of the time it was too hard for her. We were four years old when she finally started to talk again and interact with all of us. My papà did everything he could to help her and to still be with Dom and me. My zio's took us places too, practices, games. And then there was my Zia Rosaura, she stepped in and always made sure we knew how much our mam loved us. But it was a really difficult year. Hell, it was a difficult childhood. Their absence always hung over all of us."

I can feel Sebastiano's sadness and I wish I could take it away. I understand more now about why he's never really let anyone in. It makes me feel even more special that he chose me to be with and to share all of this with me. I just hope I'm not too broken for him.

"You're the first woman I've ever wanted to be with for more than one night. When the twins were taken, it always felt like there was a part of me that was missing. Finding you has helped take away that feeling of loss and I wake up everyday hoping that you haven't changed your mind," he says softy.

I never realized that there was such vulnerability inside Sebastiano until now. He always seemed so strong and confident. I take his chin and make him look at me. "You helped me heal. I thought that the life I was living was all I had, with nothing to look forward to for the rest of my days. You rescued me and made me see that I'm worth more than that. That I'm worthy of real love. The kind of love that doesn't come with hurting. I feel so protected and cherished, yet I also feel like I have the room to soar and accomplish anything."

His eyes have a sheen to them with the tears he's holding back. I want to help him heal just like he's helped me.

Sebastiano

This woman. I don't know what I did to deserve her, but I know I'll never let her get away. I kiss her and make sure she knows exactly how I feel about her.

I lay on my back trying to catch my breath and hear Schuyler giggling next to me.

"What's so funny, cuore mio?"

"You do that thing with your tongue and holy fuck, I forget everything else."

I laugh. "'I'm glad you like that, amore. But if that's the only part you remember? Then I'm doing something wrong." I look at her and arch my eyebrow. She laughs even more, holding her stomach.

It feels like a little more weight has lifted off of me after telling her about what happened when we were little. Dom and I had a great life, but there was always something missing. The emptiness that was inside of me disappeared the day we found Enzo and Gia. But the pain lingers. Finding Schuyler has started to heal those places that were hurting—I'm not sure if I'll ever completely heal, but I'm sure as hell going to try.

Chapter Fourteen

Conrad Blackwell

Tomorrow's the day.

Those entitled, bastard Mancinis think I've given up looking for my boy. They're all fucking idiots. They think I've just accepted the fact that Blaine disappeared. But I know they did something to him and I'm going to find out what. I want them to think that I gave up, when in reality, I've been preparing for tomorrow this whole time. The day I find my son and get rid of all those who've been involved. My plan will be set in motion in the morning. Having money helps to make things happen, and I will spend every last fucking dime I have to find Blaine. I'll make them feel my pain. The things they hold closest will be taken from them.

My damn wife has been more annoying than usual.

Crying and carrying on about how much she misses Blaine. Like I don't fucking miss my boy too. Maybe I'll have her taken care of along with the Mancinis and that whore Schuyler. I smile at myself in the mirror and see my stunning girlfriend coming towards me. I turn and kiss her, then take her to bed.

Tomorrow is the day I find my son. The Mancinis will pay for everything they've done to us.

Chapter Fifteen

Sebastiano

I woke up today with an ominous feeling. It's one of those things that you can't put your finger on, yet you know something bad is going to happen. I look over at Schuyler, I hope it isn't about her. I carefully wrap my arms around her, she sighs and snuggles into me.

I slowly run my hand down her stomach and hear her moan softly. And just like that, I'm instantly hard, her moan is all it takes. I slide a finger into her as I rub my cock on her from behind.

"Baby," she whispers, reaching back and stroking me.

"I need to be inside you," I growl softly and nip her ear.

She helps guide my cock into her and I slowly push it in. "Fuck, amore."

I move slowly, listening to her moans. "Stop teasing me, Bastian," she gasps.

"I don't know what you're talking about." I continue to move slowly because I know that it drives her fucking wild. I can feel her clenching my cock, it's her way of showing me who's boss. Fuck me.

"Oh God yes. Fuck me please," she cries out.

I can't hold back anymore and I slam into her faster. I feel her come all over my cock, clenching me harder than before. "Fuck, Schuyler!" I growl as I come. I hold her tight, trying to catch my breath.

"Now that's the best way to wake up." She giggles, sounding out of breath herself.

I squeeze her tighter and laugh. "I'll plan on waking you up this way for the rest of our lives."

We snuggle for a few minutes. "I was thinking maybe we should go and stay at my parents' house after your shift. We can camp out by the lake like you wanted."

"That would be perfect. Do you want to leave as soon as I get home?"

"Sure, less traffic that early in the morning."

I watch her get up and head to the bathroom. I don't think life could be any more perfect. I take that back—it'll be perfect when Schuyler's my wife and carrying my child.

Conrad has stopped harassing the police chief for now and it's kind of making me nervous because men like him don't give up. I wish I knew what his endgame was, because I know he has one. He's still telling anyone that will listen to him that I'm to blame for his son's disappearance.

Schuyler

I hum to myself while I'm showering. Then it hits me. I'm late. I quietly step out to grab my phone and look at my calendar. Fuck. I'm a month late. How did I not notice this? I start to panic...I've never been late before. What if he gets mad? What if he thinks I did this to trap him? And how am I going to get a test without Nico seeing it?

I get back in the shower and finish up. I stare at myself in the mirror, making a decision. If I'm pregnant and he doesn't want the baby, I'll raise it on my own. It'll be harder than when it was just Mira and me, but I can do it.

I slip out of the bathroom, and into our closet. I'm trying to be quiet because I can hear Sebastiano snoring lightly and I don't want to wake him just yet. Sighing softly, I get my clothes on and look down at my belly. I can do this. But first, I need to be sure.

"Baby? I have to go," I say softly, kissing his cheek.

He moans softly and grabs a hold of me. "Already?" He pouts.

"Yeah it's three-fifteen. And I want to grab coffee

for Cap and Rhys."

"Okay, amore, take some money from my wallet."

"I have money, Bastian." I chuckle.

"I know you do. But I want to pay for it. You keep your money for your own stuff," he says, looking at me.

"Okay, thank you. I love you."

"I love you more."

He pulls on some sweatpants and follows me out to the kitchen where Nico is waiting.

"Time to go," Nico says.

"Be safe. I'll see you for lunch," Sebastiano says, then kisses me.

"Have a good day, baby."

"Are you alright?" Nico asks.

"I'm good. I'm not sure I've thanked you for keeping me safe. I really appreciate it."

He nods. "You're important to the Mancinis and especially Sebastiano. It's my honor to be your guard." He pulls into the Starbucks parking lot and parks. Right as he opens his door to get out, a guy pushes past him and Nico falls back into the car. He looks a little dazed.

"Are you okay, Nico?" I frown.

He slumps over before he can answer me. "NICO!" I scream and pull my phone out. Before I can call Sebastiano, I'm yanked out of the car and blindfolded. I try to kick and scream, but a huge hand covers my mouth. Why is no one coming to help? We're in a fucking public parking lot!

"Stop screaming or this won't turn out well for

you," A man with a heavy Russian accent says in my ear.

"Fuck you. Let me go or you'll fucking regret this," I snarl as best I can with his meaty hand covering my mouth.

He laughs. "No one is coming to save you. Your man is too stupid to even know what's going on."

I get thrown in the trunk of a car. He stuffs a cloth in my mouth and puts some duct tape over it. Then he ties my hands and feet. I'm trying to stay calm and think straight. Cap will call Sebastiano when I don't show up for my shift. And he knows which Starbucks I always stop at. For once I'm glad I told him I was stopping for coffee. Nico...Oh God Nico, please don't be dead. I choke back a sob remembering how he fell back into the car so fast.

Why would someone want to take me and hurt Nico? Could this be about Blaine? It can't be, Enea said no one outside the family knows what happened. I know Sebastiano will never stop looking for me. I just hope he finds me before it's too late.

The car finally stops and my kidnapper pulls me out of the trunk. He throws me over his shoulder and carries me into a building. Or at least I think it's a building, I heard him open a door.

"Perfect timing," I hear a man say. His voice sounds oddly familiar, but I can't seem to place it.

"She's a feisty one. I would be careful," the asshole carrying me says in his thick accent.

"Well then, she can stay tied up. It'll make my

point clearer."

I heard clicking like he's taking pictures. What the fuck? Is he expecting a ransom for me? I don't have any fucking money.

"This'll show those Mancini bastards who's really in charge." He laughs.

Then it hits me. I know that voice. It's Conrad Blackwell. I start shaking. This is about Blaine. Even dead, he's making my life hell. And from the sound of it, his dad has gone crazy.

"You need someone to come take the body away?" I hear the Russian ask.

"No, not right now. Maybe later," Conrad cackles.

Holy fuck, he's killed someone?

The Russian man is talking. "Fydor and Oleg will stay to help you with security."

Their voices get softer like they're walking away. What the hell does he mean he's leaving Fydor and Oleg? Who the fuck are Fydor and Oleg? And how long is Conrad planning on holding me? I will myself not to cry. Conrad will not fucking break me. Blaine never broke me and his father sure as fuck won't either.

Sebastiano

My alarm goes off at six, I stretch and run my hand over Schuyler's side of the bed. I wish she was still sleeping beside me. My phone starts ringing.

"Hello?" I answer.

"Hey Sebastiano, it's Cap. Is Schuyler okay? I don't remember her saying she was taking the day off and she's not answering her phone."

I shoot out of bed.

"What do you mean? She left at three-fifteen this morning. She and Nico were going to stop at Starbucks and then head to the station."

"Well she never showed up. And she's never just not shown up for work. Is it the same Starbucks she always goes to?"

I'm brushing my teeth and trying to get dressed at the same time, talking to Cap on speaker.

"Yes! She said coffee, then work. I'm going to the Starbucks. I'll call you from there. And call me if she shows up."

"Okay," he says, sounding more worried.

I hang up on him and pound on Dom's door.
"HOLY FUCK, WHAT?" he yells from the other

side.

I open his door. "I need you to come with me. Something's wrong. Schuyler and Nico left at three-fifteen. She said she was going to stop at Starbucks, then head to the station. But Cap just called me and said they never showed up." As I'm explaining all this to him, he's already up and getting dressed.

"Okay. Let's go, I'm driving," he says.

"The fuck you are."

"You're in no condition to drive, asshole," he says, grabbing the keys from me.

I know he's right. But I don't have to agree with him.

The whole ride there I keep trying to call her phone and Nico's. It just keeps going to voicemail.

"FUCK!" I yell.

"We'll find her, fratello. I promise you. Maybe their car broke down and her phone died."

"Nico has a fucking phone too. Both are going straight to voicemail. What if something happened to them? Conrad has been really quiet lately and we both know that man won't quit."

My heart hurts thinking that something could've happened to Schuyler and Nico.

"Drive faster!" I snap at Dom.

We pull into the Starbucks parking lot and I see Schuyler's M8. I jump out of the car before Dom can park.

"Bastian! Fuck!" he yells. He parks as fast as he can and runs over to me.

I'm looking in her car and see Nico. "NICO!" I yell

as I pound on the window. I pull my keys out and unlock the door. I put my fingers on Nico's neck, checking for a pulse. I breathe a small sigh of relief when I feel it. "Fuck! Dom? Can you go inside and ask if they've seen her?" I say while trying to wake Nico.

"Of course. Call Papà, get him down here. Sal too," he says.

I nod and call our papà first.

"Figlio, is everything alright?" he answers.

"Schuyler's missing," I blurt out.

"What do you mean missing?"

"Cap called and said she never showed up for her shift this morning. And she mentioned she was going to stop at Starbucks. So Dom drove us here and her car is here but she's not. And I can't wake Nico up. He's breathing, but I can't wake him."

"Stay calm, Bastian. I'm sending Elio and Enzo to help you. I don't want you or Nico driving. We'll find her, figlio. We need a plan and we don't need the police involved. I'll call Sal and let him know. But first things first, get back to your house and have Gia look at Nico."

"Sì, Papà." I take a deep breath after I hang up and wait for Elio and Enzo.

When Dom went inside, they said they hadn't seen her today. They know her because she comes in before almost every shift.

I see Enzo pulling into the parking lot.

Nico finally started to wake up while we were waiting and he's pissed. He said he heard the guy who bumped into him say something in Russian and before he could even warn Schuyler, he must've passed out.

Sal shows up right after Enzo and Elio.

"I'll drive Schuyler's car and meet you at your house," Elio says.

"I'm okay to drive, Elio." Nico frowns.

"No, it's better if you don't. We don't know what they gave you," he responds.

Sal nods. "I'm off in thirty minutes and I'll head straight there."

While we're driving to our house, I call the rest of the family.

"Do you think this is Conrad that's doing this?" I ask my twin. I'm barely holding onto my sanity.

"I don't know, fratello. I wish I had the answers for you. But I do know that if this is Conrad's doing? He'll be joining his son very soon."

I nod. "I'll do it myself. This time I won't let Elio take care of it. Nico could've died. This is on me."

"This is no one's fault, Bastian. If anyone's to blame, it's whoever took her."

I sit and brood. This is the second time someone I love has been taken, first my siblings and now my Schuyler. Maybe I'm cursed. After we find her, maybe I should set her free. That would keep her out of danger. My heart hurts thinking of a life without her. But if that's what will save her, I'll do it. I'll do anything to keep her safe.

When we get home, we see everyone starting to arrive. Gia and Rella come running over to me and hug me tight.

"We're going to find her." Gia sobs as she holds me tight.

"How did you get here so fast?" I ask my parents.

"We were on our way to pick Rowan up. Now let's get inside and figure out our next move," my papà says.

We all follow him inside. I feel like my heart is dying as I think of who could have taken Schuyler and if she's okay.

"Could this be Conrad?" Dom says after we all sit down.

"That would be my guess," Sal answers.

"Then let's get out there and find that fucking bastard!" I slam my hand on the table. Rowan screams from the noise. Fuck. I go over to Gia, taking him from her. "I'm sorry, amore," I whisper as I rock him. "Zio didn't mean to scare you."

Everyone's talking about where we should start. In

the meantime, I get Rowan calmed down and Declan takes him from me.

"Let's start at Conrad's house," Luca suggests.

"We can't just go over there without a reason," Enzo responds.

"Why the fuck not?" I snap at him.

"Enzo is right, Bastian. Without a reason, he'll say we're harassing him and this will get bad fast," Sal says.

I frown at both of them, my heart still racing. Who's fucking side are they on, anyway?

"We're all on your side Bastian and you know it, so stop being an asshole. That's not helping this situation," Dom snaps back at me. I glare at my twin even though I know he's right. This twin bond is fucking annoying sometimes.

"I'm going to head down to the station and see if there's any cameras in that area that could've caught what happened. We also need to file a missing persons report. So you should come with me, Bastian. But you need to be level-headed when we go in or you'll make things worse." Sal stares at me when he talks.

"Are you listening, figlio?" my mam barks at me. The tone in her voice is telling me how irritated she's getting with my attitude.

I take my crap down a notch as I nod at my mam. "Sì, Mam. Mi dispiace."

She comes over and embraces me. "I know you're scared, amore. But we won't stop till she's back home with us. Now you need to do what Sal tells you and then we can plan our next step." She releases me and looks at my papà. "I think we need to call Giacomo Bastianini. They can help us look for her."

Giacomo "Forza" Bastianini is the head of the Cimaruta MC, Chicago chapter. We own a couple of businesses with them and are in the process of bringing them on to co-own/manage Luminescence, a male strip club. He and his club are trying to do things the lawful way like we are. But like us, they still have people they can call in times like this.

"That's a great idea, colomba mia," my papà says as he's pulling his phone out to make the call.

I take a deep breath and slowly let it out. I walk over to Gia and put my hand on her shoulder. "I'm so sorry I scared Rowan."

She gets up and hugs me. "Do you remember what you told me when we first came back to live here?"

I shake my head no.

"You told me that family always takes care of family. None of you gave up hope when Enzo and I were taken. And look how that turned out. Don't give up now. I've got you, fratello. Just like you had me then. Mancinis are forever. For always."

Everything I've been bottling up is rising fast and threatening to spill over. Damn Gia. I do remember saying that to her. She was so scared of everything when she first came back and it killed me that she thought she was alone.

Now it's my turn to take the help my family's offering. To remember that I don't have to do this alone. I'm a Mancini and it's okay to need help.

Chapter Sixteen

Schuyler

I've lost track of time. I'm worried that I might be pregnant and try to stay as calm as I can. But it's not working very well, all I can think about is what if I am pregnant and I lose the baby? How will Sebastiano know where to find me? I feel a tear slip down my cheek. My heart knows he won't stop looking for me, but I don't want him to get hurt doing it. Nico. He might be dead because of me.

I hear footsteps getting closer and a door opening. Then someone's taking my blindfold off. It takes a minute for my eyes to adjust to the light. When I finally get them to focus, I see Conrad Blackwell. And there's no body in the room with me...Did they move it? Or was there never a body?

"Where is Blaine?" he demands.

I stare at him. Does he really think I can answer him with a gag and duct tape on my mouth?

He raises his hand to slap me and I stare right into his eyes.

He cackles. "I guess you can't answer me with that in your mouth. Maybe I should replace it with something else." He rubs himself as he leers at me.

Oh God please no. I will bite off anything he puts near my mouth. He rips the duct tape off and pulls the cloth out of my mouth.

"I'll ask you one more time. Where. Is. My. Son?"

I swallow and try to wet my tongue. "Why do you think I know where he is?" My throat is dry and my voice comes out raspy.

He raises his hand again, this time slapping me across the face.

"I know you and those Mancini fucks know where Blaine is. And if you want to live, you'll tell me."

I snort. "You can do whatever you want to me, but I don't know where he is. I haven't seen him in over three months." I mean, it's not a lie. I haven't seen him since that night he tried to kill me. I don't care what Conrad does to me, I'll never betray the Mancini's. NEVER.

Sebastiano

It's been seven hours since Schuyler disappeared.

SEVEN FUCKING HOURS. Salvatore and I went to the police station and filed a missing persons report. One of the perks of him being a police officer is that he has the resources to fast-track her case. He got the okay from his captain to take lead on this as long as he doesn't let it get out of hand. He has to do this by the book. I want to throw the fucking book out.

We start by seeing if there's any cameras in the area and get lucky. There's a camera across the street that points towards Starbucks. I'm sitting in the back seat of the police car like a criminal while I wait for Sal and his partner Mac to talk to the owner of the camera. I think he stuck me back here on purpose. Asshole.

My phone buzzes in my pocket and I see a text in our family chat.

Giovanna: Any updates?

Sebastiano: Not yet. Sal and Mac are talking to a store owner. We saw a camera that looks like it's pointed at the Starbucks parking lot

Fiorella: We're going to find her

Domenico: And if it's Conrad that took her (knife emoji)

Sebastiano: More like this (gun emoji)

> Lorenzo: The Mancini in me is saying fuck yes. But the lawyer in me is saying let's arrest him and make sure he goes to federal prison…gen pop (angel and devil emoji)

> Giovanna: I checked Nico out and found a scratch on his arm. Looks like that's how they got him. He won't go to the hospital to draw blood so we don't know what they gave him. He's such a stubborn ass. No wonder he fits in with us

> Niccolò: You know I'm in this chat too right? (eyerolling emoji)

> Gianluca: *snicker* Busted

> Giovanna: What are you, five? Or maybe one too many hits with a baseball? (baseball and tongue emoji) And yes, Nico. Of course I know you're in this chat. DUH

> Domenico: The Cimaruta guys are coming to our house. Papà said be back in one hour if you can

> Sebastiano: Okay I'll let Sal know. Thanks

I shake my head and chuckle at my family. I don't know what I would do without them right now. They're the only thing that's keeping me sane. Sal said he had a patrol car go by Conrad's house. No one was there and they're staying until he gets back. I have a gut feeling Conrad's behind this. No one else would be crazy enough to come after one of us.

I'm feeling better knowing the Southside guys and the Cimaruta are on their way. We should be able to cover more ground and find my baby sooner. She better be unharmed or I will make him suffer.

We're back at my house with Cap, Lynn, Mira, and the rest of my family. It's been three more hours since Schuyler went missing. Ten hours. Where the fuck is she? Is she okay? It's killing me to think that something has happened to her and she could be hurt. I refuse to think that she could be gone. Fate wouldn't be that cruel...would it? It's like life is telling me I don't deserve to be happy—that I'm a failure.

The Southside guys are checking out Conrad's properties and the Cimaruta are waiting here with us. They're a different kind of MC. Giacomo has his family on his council, his wife Caitríona, sons Celestino and Francesco, daughters Isabella and Luciana. They've also brought the rest of their council to help, one of them is Luciana's husband, Rónán O'Callaghan. They have a son, Grayson, he's the same age as Rowan. It's their family dynamic that made my papà want to be in business with them. Family's the center of what they do, who they are and why they do things. Our family is the same way.

Giacomo turns to my papà. "Give us the story of how we got here."

My papà tells them what we know. Even the parts about what happened to Blaine.

"So you think that this Conrad, Blaine's father, is the one who took your girl?" Isabella asks.

"I can't think of anyone else that would dare come after a Mancini. As far as I know, she didn't have any enemies and Blaine made sure she never had friends," I explain.

"Do you really think he would take her to a place he owns? Could he really be that stupid?" Caitríona asks.

"We don't know." My mam sighs.

"You should look into getting trackers put in." We all turn and look at Luciana.

"You mean trackers on us?" Gia corrects her. "Like for our phones?"

"No. In you. When I was kidnapped, I was found right away because of my tracker. We all have them," Luciana explains, showing us the spot on her arm where the implant was put in. There's nothing to see besides a tiny scar.

"Seriously? Doesn't that make you feel weird? Like you have no freedom? I mean no disrespect, Giacomo, but it seems a bit extreme to inject trackers into your family." Gia sounds offended for them.

"We voted as a council to do this. It wasn't forced on us. And it saved my life. So no, I don't feel weird about having it. I don't even want to know what would've happened if I didn't. The man who kidnapped me planned to take me to England. If I didn't have a tracker? I might not be here right now."

Rónán pulls her into his arms while she's talking. I

can see the hurt in his eyes, he could've lost the love of his life. My look mirrors his, I could lose Schuyler forever. I will rain fire down on the one who took her and if they kill her? I will bring them back and kill them again. It'll be so fucking slow that they will feel every slice, every punch...Every. Fucking. Thing.

After we find Schuyler and this is over, I'm going to bring up this tracker idea again. Because if it'll help save any of us? I would do it, no questions asked. Never again do I want to feel the way I did growing up. Losing family members is not something I care to repeat.

My heart hurts watching all the couples comfort each other. I need to do something, I can't just fucking stay here and wait.

Standing up, Giacomo says, "We're going to ride around the city. You'd be surprised what you can learn just by riding. Celestino, Isabella, Brennan, and Valentino—you take the north side. Francesco, Luciana, Liam, and Rónán—the west side. Connor, Fintan, Elio, and Marco—the east side. The rest of us will take the south side."

"Let me come with you, please. I can't just sit here." I stand up and face Giacomo.

"Figlio...," my papà warns.

"It's okay, Enea. He can come with me. I'll make sure he's safe. I understand his frustration about waiting. When my Luciana was taken I thought I was going to go crazy."

My papà nods at Giacomo. "Grazie."

"Well if you're going, then we go too," Dom says as the rest of my family nods.

Giacomo pairs us up with his guys. Gia, Rella, Mam, Caitríona, and their guards stay back in case Schuyler comes home. We also have to make sure baby Rowan and baby Grayson stay safe.

Before we leave, my papà pulls me to the side.

"Are you okay, figlio?"

It feels like he's looking into my soul.

"It's okay if you aren't. Schuyler's a strong woman. She's been through a lot and she made it. I know you're worried about her. But I believe that she'll come out of this and be okay—because she has you, and you have us."

I take several deep breaths as my papà hugs me tight.

Mancinis always take care of our own.

Schuyler

I keep drifting in and out of consciousness. Each time I wake up, my hand goes to my belly. This time when my eyes open, I force myself to stay awake. I notice that someone has been in here because I see a sandwich and a bottle of water.

I look around and realize that I'm not tied up anymore. I sit up and stretch as my stomach grumbles at me. I cautiously sniff the sandwich and examine the bottle of water. It doesn't look like the bottle has been opened or tampered with. But the sandwich? I can't be sure, and I'm not hungry enough to take the chance yet.

There are no windows. But I can feel cool air coming through the vents. There's a bathroom with no mirror in it, just a toilet and a sink. Do they think I'd break a mirror and use it as a weapon? I mean of course I would, but it's scary that they've thought this through. After trying the door, I sit back down on the bed. The door's locked, like I knew it would be. There's a deadbolt on it too.

"I see you're awake," says a disembodied voice.

I whip my head around, trying to find the speaker. I finally spot it on the ceiling next to a red blinking light I'm guessing is a camera. Perverts.

"You should eat the sandwich. You must be hungry."

Whoever is talking to me has an accent. Sounds Russian. I look at the floor and frown. Sebastiano won't stop looking for me. I know that deep in my soul. The question is how long will it be before he can figure it all out?

I lay back down on the bed and face the wall. I won't let them see me cry.

Chapter Seventeen

Sebastiano

It's been three fucking days since Schuyler went missing. I feel helpless and angry. Everyone's been staying at our house and Gia's house. Southside and the Cimaruta said they'll stay as long as it takes to find her. I don't want to lose hope, but every day she's missing, my heart feels heavier.

We've spent the last three days riding all over Chicago. None of Conrad's properties checked out and it looks like he hasn't been home either. His wife seems to be missing as well. Mario and two of the Cimaruta guys—Brennan and Massimo—have been taking shifts watching Conrad's house.

Since no one has seen or heard from Conrad or Monica Blackwell, Salvatore has been given the green light to launch a full missing persons investigation for Schuyler. And the primary suspect is Conrad because of his threats and our restraining orders.

Elio comes bursting into my house calling for everyone to gather.

"I think we have a lead on Schuyler. Liam was at the grocery store and heard someone say the name Conrad. He had a Russian accent. Liam has been tailing him for the last thirty minutes. He thinks he's part of the Russian mafia here. Do any of you know if Conrad has ties to them?"

"I've never heard of him being involved with any criminal entities," my papà answers. My zios all agree with my papà.

"He was always saying how he would never have invested with us if we were doing anything illegal," Zio Leo says.

"Well maybe losing his son made him snap?" Sal suggests. "Or maybe he was always involved with them and no one knew. He is part Russian." Everyone turns to look at Sal who shrugs his shoulders. "What? I did some digging on him. His parents came from Russia around the same time Nonno and Nonna came here from Italy."

Fuck. The damn Russian mafia. I never even thought that Conrad or Blaine could be involved with the mob like us.

"So what do we do now?" I ask.

Elio looks at me. "We need to wait and see if he'll lead us to Conrad or Monica. Maybe even Schuyler.

And figure out what their connection to the Russian Mafia is."

"She's been gone for three days. I can't keep sitting on my ass, doing nothing," I snap.

"I understand, Bastian, but there's no other way. Now that we have this lead, I'll head back to the station and get as much info on them as I can." Sal comes over and hugs me. "We're going to find her. Don't ever doubt that. Conrad wants to know what happened to Blaine. I don't think he'll hurt her before he finds that out."

I nod and look at everyone. I can actually see some hope in their eyes.

"This is a good thing, figlio," Papà says.

Giacomo pulls his phone out and answers it. We hear him talking to Liam. It makes me anxious while we wait for him to tell us what he knows.

"I'm putting you on speaker," he says into the phone.

"I've been following this guy. He drove to a warehouse and went inside. He's been in there the past twenty minutes. There's three cars here." Liam rattles off the three license plates, Sal writes them down.

"I'm going to the station to run these plates and see what I can dig up. Keep me posted," he says as he's running out the door.

I slump down in my chair. "I need to do something," I say to no one in particular. "There must be somewhere we can go. I can help Liam keep an eye on the warehouse."

"Bad idea, Bastian." Elio's shaking his head. "You're

too close to this. If you see Conrad, do you think you can restrain yourself from taking him out before we can find out where Schuyler is?"

I open my mouth to argue with Elio, but the look I get from my papà has me snapping my mouth shut. Maybe I can sneak out when they're not paying attention.

"What about the thermal imaging camera?" Celestino Bastianini asks his papà.

I whip my head around to look at them.

Giacomo nods. "Take it and meet up with Liam. We can see how many people are in the warehouse."

"Wait, thermal imaging camera?" I frown at them. They're starting to pull gear from their bags. Who the fuck are these guys? I thought they were going legit like us? Okay, mostly legit. At the same time, I'm thanking God that they're here.

"That's how they found me," Luciana says softly. "After tracking me down, they used it to see into the house where I was being held. There were five heat signatures, and they were able to figure out which one was me."

"When we stormed in, we knew that the one lying on a bed had to be Luciana," Francesco Bastianini explains.

It's finally sinking in. We could actually find Schuyler, she could be in that warehouse.

"Please, I need to go with you." I'm not above begging. I need to be there when they find her.

"Let's get a better idea of who's in there and how

many. Then we can make a plan to go in," Giacomo says. "We'll be ready to go when Liam says so."

I take a deep breath. Logically, I know he's trying to fucking help me, but I can't stay here. I feel my mam come and stand beside me.

"I know how hard it is to wait, amore. But you have to trust everyone here to do their jobs," I hear her say to me.

My shoulders sag. "I know, Mam, but I can't just do nothing," I choke out.

She wraps me in a hug. One of those hugs that only your mam can give you.

"We're going to find her," she whispers as she holds me.

With everything my mam has gone through, she still has so much love and hope in her. My sister is just like her, and so is Schuyler. The women in my life are everything to me, and I won't stop till Schuyler is back in my arms and every one of those bastards involved in her kidnapping is dead. Every. Fucking. One.

We've been waiting for an hour now. An hour that's felt like an eternity.

Giacomo answers his phone on speaker.

"There are ten heat signatures at the warehouse. One alone in a room, two outside that room, three in another room, and four walking the outside perimeter. They've rotated two times now. Every hour. I've seen two of their faces clearly, definitely Russian mob."

Giacomo sighs. "Fuck. Okay, you and Tino keep watching. We're headed to you now."

"Okay, one of us will text if anything changes," Liam says before hanging up.

"We should take the cars," my papà says. "We have enough for everyone. I want you and the girls to stay here, colomba mia. Please."

My mam frowns, but nods.

"Columba mia, I can't have you all there. I won't be focused," he says softly to her, pulling her into his arms.

"I know, amore. Please be careful and bring everyone home safe."

"Since no one will ask, I have to," Gia says. "What if Schuyler isn't in there? No one has seen her yet."

"We're willing to take the risk. If she's not, we keep looking," Elio says as the others nod.

I am so fucking grateful for everyone here. I hug Gia, I know it wasn't easy for her to speak up. But it had to be said.

"Okay, let's get going," Giacomo tells everyone. "If she's there, we don't want them to try and move her."

Schuyler

I don't know how long I've been in here. Because there are no windows, I can't tell when the sun rises and sets. I know someone is watching me at all times. I did try and reach that stupid speaker and blinking red light. I need to be taller.

The day they took me, I didn't touch the food. But I

had to drink some of the water. I didn't get sick so the next time they brought a sandwich I did eat some of it. They keep bringing me food and if I'm up, they tell me to back away from the door. The first time, they warned me that if I attacked the person bringing me food, I would regret it. So of course I attacked the asshole who came in. That fucker was huge. Like Nico huge. I basically bounced off him and onto the bed. Whoever was watching laughed.

Nico...I wish I knew if he was okay. He has to be okay. And Sebastiano, my soul, I miss him so damn much.

Conrad came in a few times with the behemoth dickhead. He's a pussy, just like his son. The coward knows I could take him. Every time he comes in, he asks about Blaine. I keep giving him the same blank stare. Like I said, he won't fucking break me.

After I lay back down on the bed, I hear the door open. Just as I'm turning to see who it is, my arms are restrained and tied behind me.

Sebastiano

The thirty minute drive is killing me. When we started to change the way we did business, I thought we could just leave our criminal history in the past. But I've realized that we can't. There's always going to be something that brings us back to our roots. Because whoever took Schuyler will die by my hand. I won't leave it to the rest of them like I did with Blaine. And if she's hurt? That death will be slow.

We meet up with Liam and Celestino at the property next to the warehouse.

"There's cameras at the end of the driveway. They're not hiding them. But we scouted the property and there seems to be no surveillance towards the back. I don't think they thought it through if they're using this as a base," Liam informs us.

Elio passes out the earpieces that we'll be using.

"We'll go in threes to use the thermal imaging camera so that everyone can see what we're up against." We all nod at Giacomo.

"I haven't seen anyone leave since I've been here. But I feel like we need to hurry," Celestino says.

"I agree," says Massimo.

Everyone puts their kevlar vests on and we all make sure we have enough ammo for our guns. It takes about fifteen minutes for everyone to take turns using the thermal imaging camera.

Elio then separates us into four groups. There are four doors into the warehouse. So we're evenly split with someone from each of the clans. My group includes Nico, Massimo, Francesco, and Sal. We'll be taking the door on the left side. Schuyler has to be in there.

We see two more cars drive up and park. Four more men climb out and go into the warehouse. Fuck. The odds are becoming less in our favor as more show up. Let's hope that's all of them.

Schuyler

The walking pile of shit takes me to another room and ties me to a chair. After a few minutes, another asshole comes in with Conrad.

"You have one more chance to tell me where my son is. I know the fucking Mancinis had something to do with his disappearance. And I know it's because of you. You're a cheap whore and I wish my son had never met you. Now, WHERE. IS. HE?"

Little flecks of spit are flying towards me and it's making me gag. I stare at him with the same look I've been giving him this whole time. I see him nod at asshole number two, who comes towards me and smacks me across the face.

I laugh. "You can't even hit me yourself? Pussy." I turn to asshole number two. "And you? You like hitting women? You'll find out what happens if you do it again. By the way, you hit like a little girl."

Conrad starts laughing. "You think you're untouchable because you're fucking that stupid Mancini boy? He's at the bottom of their hierarchy. You picked poorly."

I roll my eyes at him. No wonder Blaine was so

stupid, this is what he had to look up to. Suddenly I feel sorry for him. But just a little. And now it's gone.

"Again," Conrad snaps at asshole two.

This time he punches me. But nothing will compare to what Blaine did to me that night. So I don't show them any fear. I think of Sebastiano's handsome face, his beautiful blue-green eyes. His smile that melts my heart every time I see it. His arms around me, making me feel protected and loved. Nothing can truly hurt me again, now that I know what it's like to be with my soulmate. I smile, thinking of him holding me, telling me how much he loves me, and I feel no pain.

Sometime during my daydream, I pass out from that neanderthal hitting me. In the blackness, I dream about my Sebastiano. I dream he's come to rescue me. I can even hear his voice as if he's in the room with me...

Sebastiano

My group heads to the room on the left only to find it empty. That was the room where we saw two guards outside the door. But there's no one there now. We slowly make our way to the next door. Still nothing. It feels like we've been searching for hours, when in reality it's only been fifteen minutes.

After exploring two corridors, we finally get to a closed door that has muffled voices coming from behind it.

"That's Conrad Blackwell," I whisper to Massimo. I can't make out all the words, but I think I hear Conrad asking if she's dead. Who's "she"? I don't wait to find out.

I push past Nico and kick the door in. Besides Conrad, there are two other men in the room. Then I see her. I aim and shoot the guy closest to Schuyler. Nico grabs Conrad as he's trying to run, and Francesco gets the other guy. I go straight to Schuyler—she's not moving and my heart drops. I scoop her up gently and bring her to my chest.

"Cuore mio. Please wake up," I murmur, kissing her temple. "Please."

It takes what feels like hours before she barely whispers, "Sebastiano?"

Relief floods my body at hearing her voice. "I'm here, amore. Please, open those beautiful blue eyes for me."

She slowly complies. I wipe some of the blood off her face and I'm relieved to see it's not like last time. She took some good hits and now I wish I hadn't shot that fucker. He should be in that room with Conrad and the other assholes that didn't get fucking shot.

"We need to get you to the hospital." I look at her and she sniffles.

"I knew you'd come for me," she whispers hoarsely.

"I'll always come for you, cuore mio. You're mine forever."

She starts to cry as she clings to me. I pick her up and carry her out of the room. Nico comes running back to us.

"Is she okay?" he asks.

Schuyler lifts her head and looks at Nico.

"Oh Nico, you're okay—I was so worried." She sobs.

He leans over and kisses her head. He's lucky I trust him. Plus, he did get hurt protecting Schuyler. Or else I would be ripping his lips off.

Chapter Eighteen

Sebastiano

With Gia's help, we finally get Schuyler to agree to go to the hospital. She's even more stubborn than I am. And now Gia and I are standing in the waiting room. I'm beginning to seriously fucking hate waiting for things.

"I need you to stay with Schuyler tonight," I say to Gia. "I have to be there when they talk to Conrad."

"Mam's going to bring Rowan here. Zia, Rella, and the Cimaruta women are coming with her. We'll all be here with Schuyler."

"Thank you, Gia. For everything you've done for Schuyler and for me."

"I would do anything for you, Bastian. And for Schuyler too."

I stand up when I see the doctor coming out.

"How is she? Can we see her?" I blurt out before he can get a word out.

He chuckles at me. "They're both fine and you can see her soon."

Okay. I know I've had a long fucking few days but I swear the doctor said "they". Who the fuck is "they"?

Gia's staring at him too. "They?"

Oh good, I'm not crazy. Gia heard the same thing that I did.

"Schuyler and the baby, they're both fine. I would like to monitor them for a day or two. She has a concussion and she's a little dehydrated."

Holy fuck. Schuyler's pregnant? Why didn't she tell me?

"The nurse will be out once they get her situated. I'll be back to check in with you later."

I watch him walk away, then turn to my sister, "I'm not crazy, am I? You heard him too, right? He said she's pregnant?" I whisper to her.

She nods at me with wide eyes. "Maybe she just found out? I don't think she would keep that from you, Bastian. Are you okay?"

I think I'm nodding at her. At least that's what it feels like. Or maybe it's my whole body twitching? I don't fucking know right now. But Schuyler's carrying my baby. This is everything I've wanted, I hope she's as happy as I am.

"Schuyler Viñales' family?" a nurse calls out.

Gia and I both stand up.

"You need to go in first," she says to me. "I'll call everyone and let them know she's okay. The baby news is for both of you to tell."

I hug Gia. "I'm going to be a papà," I say to her. She gives me the biggest smile.

I turn and follow the nurse.

I walk into Schuyler's room and go over to her. "Why didn't you tell me, cuore mio?" I ask softly after I kiss her.

She pulls back and looks at me with a puzzled look on her face. Then the color starts to drain from it. "T-tell you what?"

I place my hand on her stomach. "The baby." I lean in and kiss her again. "The doctor said you're both fine."

Her tears start falling. "I-I didn't do it on purpose. I swear I didn't. Please don't be mad. I wasn't trying to trap you."

I stare at her. Does she really think I would be mad about this? This is Blaine's doing. He made her feel like everything was her fault, all the time. I wish I could fucking bring him back and torture him even more.

"You're carrying our baby. There's nothing I can think of that would make me happier at the moment." I sit on the bed and wrap my arms around her. "This is the best news I've ever heard. You're safe. The baby's safe. We're going to be okay."

I kiss her, then her belly.

"Ciao, my bambino, I'm your papà. Your mam and I can't wait to meet you. You're going to be born into the best family ever. Your nonno and nonna are going to be so happy and you already have a cousin Rowan—I know you're going to be the best of friends. And you have lots of zios and zias. You're already one of the most loved bambinos ever."

Schuyler

I can't help smiling as I watch Sebastiano talking to my belly. The baby can't be bigger than a jelly bean and I doubt it has ears yet, but he's talking to it like it can understand him. Our baby's already so lucky, he or she is going to have the best papà.

"I realized the day that Conrad took me that I was late. I was going to take a test to make sure. And if it was positive, I was going to tell you that night."

Sebastiano's arms tighten around me and all of a sudden, my fears melt away. I can't believe I thought he'd be angry with me. He's not Blaine. I don't know what I did to deserve him and his love, but I'm so glad to have them.

"Our son's going to be best friends with Rowan," he whispers.

I giggle. "Our son? What if it's a girl?"

The look on his face is one of confusion. Like he's never considered he could have a daughter. I snort.

"Well then she's never going to leave the house.

And we'll need to have a bunch more babies so she'll at least have some friends."

I laugh at the serious look on his face. "Baby, you can't keep our daughters locked up forever."

"I sure as fuck can."

He makes a pouty face at me. It's so damn adorable.

"Our daughters won't be leaving the house, ever. We could homeschool them. Or how about tutors? Girl tutors, no boys. Yeah, that could work. No boys allowed. And then they could just live with us for the rest of their lives."

I laugh listening to him. He suddenly gets a serious look on his face.

"I hate to leave you both. But I have to go and meet the others. Gia will be here with you. My mam, Zia Rosaura and Caitríona will be here soon."

I know what he's talking about when he says he has to meet the others. Conrad will pay for what he did. And I'm guessing they'll finally tell him about what happened to Blaine.

"Nico will be here soon too. He needed some time with Conrad and the guys from the warehouse. I'll wait till he gets here."

"I'm so glad he's okay. Before that guy pulled me out of the car, all I saw was him passing out. I didn't know if he was dead or not."

I can feel my anxiety rising again. I take a few deep breaths as Sebastiano wraps his arms around me.

"Shh. It's ok, baby. You're okay. Conrad will never

come near you again," he whispers while rubbing my back.

We both look up when we hear a knock. Sebastiano says to come in, and Gia comes walking in with Nico beside her. I can see the relief on both of their faces.

Sebastiano

I don't want to leave Schuyler right now. But I swore to myself that when we found her, I would be the one to take care of those who were responsible. This is on me. They took my girl.

I wasn't the one to end Blaine's life and part of me regrets that. It feels like I didn't do enough. That I just left it for someone else to handle. That's not going to happen this time. I don't know if I can end someone's life, but I'm sure as hell going to fucking try. I almost lost not only my heart, but our baby.

Fuck. Baby. I'm going to be a papà. That thought used to send me into a sheer panic, but now? All I want to do is stay here and keep smiling like an idiot while holding Schuyler. Oh, and rub her belly till the baby pops out. I mean that's how it works, right?

Gia and Nico knock, then come in. Gia's got the same smile plastered on her face as I do. It's contagious, I swear.

Nico looks confused. It makes me smile even more.

"Why are you both smiling like you're fucking

crazy? What's the deal? Gia's had the same creepy smile the whole time we were walking up here." Nico's making faces at me and Gia, then squints at Schuyler.

Schuyler giggles and looks at me. I nudge her.

"Tell him." I chuckle. "He might cry if you don't."

That gets me a dirty look from Nico which makes me laugh even more.

"I'm pregnant," she says softly and smiles.

"Holy shit! Congrats to both of you! Wait, it is yours, right?"

That shithead is looking at me, smirking.

"I knew I should've left you in the car." I laugh.

"Seriously though, I'm so glad you're both okay." As he's saying this, we can hear the emotion in his voice. "I don't know what I would've done if—I'm so sorry."

"It's not your fault, Nico. You couldn't have done anything differently," I say to him. He looks like he doesn't believe me. We both feel like we failed Schuyler. But really, the only failure here is me. And I'm going to fix that.

"I didn't even see anyone till that guy dragged me out of the car. There's no way you could have prevented that," Schuyler says to Nico.

"I was supposed to make sure no one got near you. I failed. But I swear to both of you, all three of you, that it will never happen again."

I know how he feels, but those guys were professional criminals. They knew what they had to do and how to do it. I will never blame him for what happened that day. No one could've foreseen it.

"Look, those guys were ready and waiting, it would've been the same if it had been me there and not you. So don't blame yourself."

Nico takes a deep breath and gives me a slight nod.

I kiss Schuyler. "I'll be back, amore. You rest and listen to Gia. She's smarter than the doctors."

Gia snorts.

Chapter Nineteen

Sebastiano

Leaving Schuyler so soon is the hardest thing I've had to do. Especially after finding out she's pregnant. But I need to see to Conrad.

I drive over to our warehouse. Everyone is here, same as last time, but with the addition of the Cimaruta MC.

I park my car and sit for a minute, thinking of all the things that have happened in the last four months. I found my soulmate and almost lost her twice. And both times it was because of a Blackwell.

When I get inside, I see everyone in the main area of the warehouse. It's odd to see Isabella and Luciana Bastianini here with everyone. In our family, the women aren't usually involved in things like this. But because they are part of the Cimaruta MC council, they're a part of everything they do.

"Are you sure you want your hand in this?" my papà asks.

I nod at him. "I need to be here. He tried to take my future from me. First Blaine tried to kill Schuyler, and now Conrad tried to take her and our baby. Schuyler's pregnant, Papà."

My papà's eyes get wide. "Congratulations, figlio. We will celebrate later. Right now, Conrad must pay for what he's done to our family. You can go in after your zio's have their time with him. We have some questions we need answered. Like why he was trying to undermine us and our business."

When we brought Conrad into Mancini Legacy, he was supposed to be a partner, like Giacomo Bastianini. But somewhere along the line, he got it in his head that we were criminals and nothing we did was legit. We need to know why.

I watch the clock on the wall. Each tick of the second hand reverberates in my head like a sledgehammer. Finally my papà steps back and I follow Elio and Giacomo to the room where Conrad is being held.

He's naked and strapped to a chair, begging for his life. I look around and see my zio's standing off to the side.

I take the plastic protectors from Mario and put them on. It feels like déjà vu. Who knew we would be facing off with Conrad the same way we did with his son Blaine.

The minute he sees me, he stops blubbering and starts screaming about Blaine. Demanding that I tell him where he is before we kill him.

"Your son is dead," Elio tells him. "In fact, he begged for his life just like you are."

"Y-you're lying," Conrad sputters out. "Blaine's not dead."

Elio glares at him. "Your son was a woman beater. Men who like him are worthless. From what we heard, he learned it from you. We found your wife. You're a fucking douchebag for beating her and leaving her to die. YOUR WIFE. She's the one person besides your children that you're supposed to cherish and protect with your life."

"You're a fucking murderer. Who are you to say that a man who can keep his woman in line is an abuser? And that he should die? You should die too! And fuck Monica. She was a lying cheating whore!" Conrad screams.

I move to stand in front of him.

"I knew you were a fucking criminal," he spits at me.

I step to the side and take the brass knuckles Giacomo offers me. I make sure they're secure on my hand before I start talking.

"You touched someone that belongs to me."

"I NEVER TOUCHED HER!" he screams.

I strike him once across the face and blood flies from his nose.

"I didn't say you could fucking speak."

I start to beat him, releasing all the fear and anger I felt when he took my Schuyler. All the tension that has built up these last few days. I pour all of that into hitting him. Sometime in this process, I trade the brass knuckles for a switchblade. I don't know when or how that happened. The next thing I'm conscious of is Elio making me stop.

"Bastian, are you sure you want to be the one to end this? This is something you can't come back from. Something that will always be with you no matter where you go. You can walk away from this right now and it will be okay. You've avenged your woman. We can take care of it from here."

I look at Elio, then grab the Glock on the table and point it at Conrad. He's still trying to beg for his life, through the blood, snot and tears that are running down his face. I don't even see him anymore. All I see is the one who tried to take my future from me.

I pull the trigger and drop the gun.

Domenico

I know Bastian needs this. I have this overwhelming need to be in there with him and make the decision to go to my twin. We've been to hell and back before.

At least now as adults, I can be here for him. There's no way I'm letting him do this alone. We've been connected since the moment we were conceived. And when the twins were taken, we still had each other.

I walk into the room right as Sebastiano grabs the Glock. I see the look in his eyes as he points it at Conrad. I walk towards him as he pulls the trigger.

When he drops the gun, I make sure I'm the first person he sees.

"Dom," is all he says.

"I got you, fratello."

He collapses into my arms. I look at Elio and Giacomo. They both nod at me—they know why Bastian had to do this. Giacomo just went through this with his daughter.

I can feel Bastian shaking. If I could take this from him, I would. But since I can't, I'm going to do everything I can to help him through it.

I can feel every bit of his anger, hurt, and relief. No matter how hard it was for him, he now has closure. Conrad and Blaine will never be able to hurt Schuyler again.

I pray that Bastian will be able to remember that when the adrenaline wears off. If he doesn't, I'll be sure to remind him.

Schuyler

I'm worried about Sebastiano, when he left he didn't look too good. I know he's blaming himself for what happened to me. Nico is too. But they need to know that there's nothing they could've done.

From what I know, Sebastiano was there with Blaine, but he wasn't the one to finish it. This time? I don't think he'll leave this to the others to take care of. I just hope he's able to come back to me after. He's the strongest man I've ever known, but something like this could break anyone.

I look over at Nico. He hasn't taken his eyes off me or the door since Sebastiano left.

"Do you think he'll be okay?" I ask him.

"Yes, I think so. He just needs to find his closure with Conrad."

"But Conrad didn't touch me."

He frowns at me. "Someone touched you, Schuyler. The evidence is on your face and body."

"It was the Russian."

"You're telling me Conrad had nothing to do with the marks on you?"

I stay quiet and stare at him.

"That's what I thought. The Russian may have done the dirty work, but Conrad was the one telling him what to do. Cause he's a fucking coward. I understand how Sebastiano's feeling. When I woke up and realized you were gone? I was ready to kill anyone who was involved."

I nod slowly. I understand what Nico is saying. It just kills me that my sweet Bastian is hurting again because of me.

Sebastiano

I did it, I avenged my girl. It was surreal, like I was there doing it, yet I wasn't. I don't really know how to feel right now. I do know I feel better because I know that Conrad and Blaine will never be able to hurt her again. Or anyone else.

We found Monica Blackwell's body in that warehouse too. She was tortured before they left her to die. Fucking cowards, they didn't have to kill her. But that's the kind of fucking shitbags they are. Woman beaters and now killers.

I hope Schuyler understands why I had to do this. Why I had to be the one to finish it.

I've never been so grateful to have my twin with me.

Chapter Twenty

Sebastiano

It's been a month since Schuyler was abducted. I've been trying to deal with all the emotions that have come back to haunt me from my childhood, triggered by her kidnapping. I know Schuyler suspects there's something going on, but I keep telling her I'm fine. Yeah, it's a lie. A big fat ugly lie. But I don't want her to think it's her fault because it isn't.

I pack a bag after Schuyler leaves for work. I don't want her to know I'm leaving. I need to go and clear my head. I need to be okay before our baby comes. I know now what my papà meant when he said he didn't want me taking care of Blaine or Conrad. But I had to do it, I had to be the one to finish it.

If it wasn't for me, Schuyler wouldn't have been

taken in the first place. Just like if I had just opened my mouth when Enzo and Gia were taken. Both times I should've been able to do something about it. Maybe I'm cursed, and if I am? I don't want my child to have to live with it too.

I leave the letter I wrote to Schuyler on her side of the bed. I know she's my life, my heart and soul. But I need to fix myself before I can be the man she needs. The father that our baby needs. I make sure that I have the picture that we took last week. It's my favorite picture of us. In it, she's leaning back on me and I'm kissing her neck. My hands are over hers on her belly. Luciana Bastianini took it when they came to visit.

I'm driving to Lake Renegade, my plan is to stay in one of the cabins. It's cold out and we have some vacancies, so I rented it anonymously. Hopefully, no one in the family will notice anything is up. And as long as I stay away from the main office, I won't bump into any of them. I even went so far as to rent a car so they won't see mine.

I stop at the grocery store to get enough supplies for about a week, maybe a little more. I don't actually know how long I'll be there, so I'll just go back to the store if I need to, I guess.

It's still dark when I get to the cabin and park, looking around before I get out of the car to make sure that no one is watching. There are a few other campers, some with RV's, three cabins are occupied, and a few crazies staying in tents. I mean, it's forty degrees out here.

I get settled in the cabin, and turn off "read receipts" on my texts. I also turn off the "find my iPhone" option. I don't shut down my phone completely, in case there's an emergency. I left Dom a note asking him to take care of Schuyler for me. Because I can't right now—I need to get my fucking shit together. I don't know how long I'll be here. Maybe a few days, maybe weeks, I just don't know.

I make sure I put our picture in the middle of the table. To remind me why I'm here hiding out like a fucking coward. I already miss her and she doesn't even know I'm gone yet.

While I unpack, I put a calendar up on the wall and circle Schuyler's doctor appointment next month, three weeks from today. We're supposed to find out the sex of the baby, she's so excited. I love going to every appointment with her and seeing the baby grow. That first time we heard it's heartbeat...that was the most incredible sound I've ever heard.

Looking around the cabin, I sigh and start putting stuff together to make dinner. Pancakes and sausages, my mam used to make that for Dom and me when we were little. Mam. She would be so disappointed in me for running away instead of coming to the family. But how do you explain how worthless you feel? How you feel like everything is your fault. That your siblings were taken because you were too scared to cry out and say something. When everything bad that has happened in your life was your fault.

Schuyler

I know something's been off with Bastian these last few weeks. I wish he would talk to me. It makes me wonder if he's changed his mind about me…or the baby. It kills me to think that maybe he's decided that this really isn't what he wants. That all the things we've been through are just too much.

"Are you okay?"

I turn and look at Nico. "Yeah, I'm okay."

"You're quiet today. Usually you're more excited about going home."

Leave it to Nico to notice my mood. He notices everyone's moods.

"I'm okay. Really." I put a smile on my face and rub my belly. "Cap's taking me off duty soon. As it is, I'm only allowed to drive." I make faces and Nico laughs.

"Well, your job isn't easy. That bambino's the most important thing now."

I smile. He's right, no matter what, this baby is everything. We're supposed to go in next month and find out if it's a boy or girl. I'm really excited to know the sex of the baby, Bastian says it doesn't matter to him if we find out—it's up to me.

Nico pulls into the garage and I head inside and straight to our room. I freeze as I look at the bed. Bastian's always in bed when I get home from my shift. The bed is made and there's an envelope propped up on the pillow. I get that sinking feeling in the pit of my stomach.

I slowly walk over to the bed and see my name on the envelope in his handwriting. I feel like I'm going to throw up and my hands are trembling as I pick it up. I sit on the bed and slowly open it…

Cuore mio,

You need to know that you and our bambino are the most important things to me. I know you're worried, but we're going to be okay.

In order for me to be the best husband to you and father to our bambinos, I need to fix my shit. I need to find a way to slay my demons.

I've been carrying around this guilt over not being able to save Gia and Enzo, and now you. I don't know how to be me anymore, and if I can't be me, how can I protect you and our bambinos? I would never survive losing any of you. I love you more than I ever thought was possible to love someone. You are my whole world.

I just need some time. I promise I'll always come back to you. You hold my heart in your hands forever.

Ti amo cuore mio,

Bastian

My hands are still shaking. Where did he go? My tears are falling on his letter when I hear a knock. I look up and see Dom standing in the doorway.

"I got a letter too," he says softly. "I never knew he felt so much responsibility over what happened with Enzo and Gia. I knew it was bad when I told them I saw Dorian leaving the room we were in. This wasn't his fault. I didn't know he saw Dorian too. I thought I was the only one."

I stand up and hug Dom. We both love Bastian so much. I know he's holding back tears.

"He said in my letter that I need to make sure you're okay and that you stay here. He doesn't know how long he'll be gone, and he doesn't want you to leave."

I nod and wipe my face. "I can't stand that he's hurting and I'm not there to help him. It wasn't his fault that Conrad took me. If it was anyone's, it was mine. I'm the idiot that stayed with Blaine for so long."

Dom frowns at me. "You're not an idiot. You were in a situation that you didn't know how to get out of. He was threatening you and Mira. If it had just been you, you would've left him, right?"

"Yes. If he hadn't threatened her, I would never have gone back to him."

Dom embraces me again. "My brother is strong. But I think he's feeling guilty that you were taken and Nico was hurt. He'll find a way past all of this. And when he does he's going to need you. He's going to need you to show him that he's not as broken as he thinks he is."

I hug Dom back. I know he's right, but I'm so damn worried about Bastian. I hate that he feels like he has to do this alone. He and I are going to have a talk when he gets back. We're a team. And now with the baby coming, we need to do this together, not alone.

"You should get some rest. I'm going to see if anyone knows where he is," Dom says softly.

"Okay. Please come and let me know if you hear anything."

Dom turns and closes the door. I look around to see if I can tell what's missing. I mean, he must've taken some things with him. I walk over to our dresser and see the picture that Luciana took of us is gone. Sebastiano always said that was his favorite picture. Other than that, I notice some clothes and his small suitcase are gone.

I lay on the bed and hold his pillow. It still smells like him. I can't stop the tears from flowing. Our appointment for the ultrasound is in three weeks. I hope he comes back before then.

I call Sebastiano's phone and it goes straight to voicemail.

"Baby, I love you so much. I wish I knew what to say to make everything alright. What happened to me was never your fault.

It was mine because I let Blaine control me for so long. You rescued me in more ways than one. I need you with me forever and I pray that there's never a time that you won't want to be with me. I'll always be here for and with you. Please come home so we can get through this together. You are my hero."

Gráinne

Getting that phone call from my Domenico broke my heart. I knew there was something wrong with my Sebastiano, but I didn't know it was this bad. First I need to go and see Schuyler, then I need to find my boy. He's blaming himself for something that was never his fault.

When Lorenzo and Giovanna were taken, I shut down. I didn't know what to do, and I was so afraid. What if I couldn't love Sebastiano and Domenico enough? I thought that if I separated myself from them, they would be better off. Enea pulled me out of that darkness and now it's my turn to help my son. Looking back, I think my inability to deal with the kidnapping hurt my older boys more than I realized at the time.

Searching the house, I find Enea where he always is. The kids started calling it his bat cave because of

Gia's husband, Declan, and the name stuck. I knock before hitting the spot on the wall that opens the door.

"Colomba mia." He smiles, then stands and comes over to me.

I hold him tight and before I know it, I'm bawling.

"What's going on?" he asks me, worry coloring his voice.

I tell him about my conversation with Domenico.

"I have to find him." I choke out a sob. "This is my fault. Not his."

"This is not your fault, colomba mia. None of what happened to our children was ever your fault."

"But I'm the one that shut down when Enzo and Gia were taken. I hurt Dom and Bastian so much."

"You did everything you could at the time. No one has ever blamed you for the way you dealt with all of it. Please, colomba mia, never blame yourself."

I look into the eyes of the man that I have loved my entire adult life. Since the day we met, his love for me has never waned, it's only grown as our family has grown.

"Where will you start to look for him?" he asks me.

"I don't know. But I'm going to see Schuyler and Dom first. Then I'll come home and figure out what to do. Where do you think he would go?"

"I wish I knew, amore. He's never just disappeared before, so I don't even know where to start. Colomba mia, you make sure to text or call and keep me in the loop. If you need me, I'll go with you."

"Thank you, amore. But I need to do this alone, I

need to fix what I did to our babies."

I park at Domenico and Sebastiano's house and knock on the front door.

"Mam." Domenico pulls me into a hug, his body is shaking.

"Amore, it's okay. I'm going to find your brother and help him see that none of this was his fault."

Schuyler comes into the living room while I'm talking and I see the pain in her eyes. I walk over to her and embrace her.

"Everything's going to be okay. My children are scarred, but they're strong. I know you love my Sebastiano and you'll help him through this too. I'm so happy that you came into his life. Into all of our lives."

"Thank you. Gráinne," she whispers. "I don't know what I did to deserve all of you, but I promise I'll never take it for granted. You're the family I've always wished for growing up. And knowing my baby will be part of the best family ever makes me even happier."

I hug Schuyler tighter. I'm so glad Sebastiano has her. They've helped each other so much these last few months. Domenico hands me the letter Sebastiano wrote him. My tears fall while I read it. I never even knew my baby was hurting so much. How did I not see it? How was I so blind and wrapped up in myself that I missed it all these years? Schuyler shows me her letter too.

"If either of you hear from Bastian, you call me. I'm heading back home and I will find him. I love you both."

"I love you, Mam," Domenico says, hugging me tight. "Drive safe. Text me when you get home."

"I will, amore." I hug them both one last time.

Time to find my boy. As I'm driving, I try to figure out where he could be. Would he come back to Lake Renegade? It's really the only place I can think of. But I didn't see his car on the streets when I drove through our town.

I make it a point to drive slowly around our town again. I worry that I've failed him. I wish I had known how he felt, maybe I could've helped him before he got to this point.

I pull over to try his cell phone again and it goes straight to his voice mail. I decide to leave him a message.

"My sweet Sebastiano, please call me back and let me know where you are and that you're okay. I need to talk to you. None of what's happened has ever been your fault. I know you feel like it is and I understand. But my sweet boy, you were never to blame for any of it. Please call me. I love you."

My heart is hurting for my oldest boy. I wish I could go back in time to when the twins were taken and do it over. I wouldn't shut down again like I did before. I would remember that my boys needed me just as much, if not more. I failed them by not realizing what I was doing to them. But now I'm determined to fix it. I need to make sure Sebastiano knows that it was never his burden to take on, and I'm so sorry that he's carried that around with him all these years.

Sebastiano

Earlier, Schuyler left me a voicemail. That woman will always hold my heart. I know she's hurting because I left. But I don't know how to explain what I'm feeling about everything that's gone on.

When my phone rings again, it's my mam. I'm not ready to talk to anyone, not even her. She's always been the center of our family. Even when she stopped talking to us, we still went to her with everything.

I see that she's left me a voicemail. My tears fall while I listen to it. The pain in her voice is killing me. I never want to be the cause of pain for any of the women in my life. I thought I would hear disappointment in her voice but there's none of that. She just sounds so sad.

I finish cooking and sit down to eat. I think I'll take a walk later tonight after it gets dark. Until then, I plan to stay inside, there's too much risk in going out— someone is bound to see me. Even future grocery shopping will have to be done outside of Lake Renegade.

Chapter Twenty-One

Schuyler

It's been almost three weeks since Sebastiano left and
the first time since we've been together that he hasn't
come to the firehouse to visit me, I had to tell Cap what
I could about what was going on. He said he
understood, and he knows that Bastian will come back.

Talking with Cap helped me see that men like
Sebastiano need to be able to fix everything and protect
the ones they love. When I was taken, it must have
made him feel useless.

I leave him a voicemail everyday and text him
whenever I think of something I want to say to him.
Which is often. I wish he would call me back or just
text me to say he's okay. It's making me more and more
nervous as time goes on. The need to help him gets

stronger with every day that passes. It's worse because no one knows where he is. No one has heard from him at all. I just need to know that he's alright. That he's safe.

I rub my belly.

"Your papà is a great man. He's just hurting right now. But when he comes back? You'll see the extraordinary man that he is. He'll lay his life down for his family and he will give you everything you could ever want or need. And all he wants in return is your love and support. So that's what we'll give him when he comes home to us. Forever."

I pray that he's back in time for my appointment tomorrow. I refuse to find out what we're having until he's back with us.

Sebastiano

Everyone has been texting me and leaving voicemails multiple times a day since I left. It's been almost three weeks and I'm no closer to feeling normal than the day I left.

I still don't know what to say to them. I can't come out sounding like a fucking scared little boy. I'm the oldest of my siblings, I'm not supposed to crumble like this. I was raised to be a strong man, to safeguard my family.

I stay quiet when I hear a knock at the cabin door.

FUCK. I forgot that my mam always comes to check on the campers that are here longer than a week. And now she's knocking on my door. I know that if I just stay quiet, she'll leave. But she'll be back again.

Maybe it's time to face her? I can't stand the thought that I've disappointed her.

Well, shit. I may not have the option to ignore her. I remember that I left something on the table outside. The one thing that I've carried with me since my childhood. The one thing that anyone in my family would know without a doubt belonged to me.

FUCK.

I quietly look out the window and watch my mam find that exact thing.

Gráinne

I've looked everywhere for my boy, it's been almost three weeks since he left. I know that everyone has been texting him and leaving voicemails like I have. I hope he's getting them.

I spend hours driving around our town everyday. I don't know why, but I have the feeling he's near. I just wish I knew where. The longer he's away, the more guilt I feel for hurting him so much as a child. It was never my intention to do that.

I head to the campgrounds to do my normal routine with the campers. I like to say hi to the ones that stay longer than a week or two. We always check on them at the beginning of their stay and also during. I feel like it's a nice touch to make sure they have everything they need.

There's one cabin that didn't answer last time and they haven't checked out yet. We'll see if they answer the door this time.

I get to the last cabin. It's one of our bigger cabins—built like a small cottage. There are three like this.

There's an SUV in the driveway that I didn't see the last time I tried to come by and say hello. That's a good sign, hopefully they're here.

I walk up to the door and look over at the table that's on the porch. There's a mug of tea, it's still steaming so I know someone's here. Right beside it, I see something that makes my heart sing.

My Bastian is here. I found my boy. I pick up the picture on the table. It was taken a week before the twins were kidnapped. In it, Sebastiano is holding Lorenzo and Domenico is holding Giovanna. My two older boys looked so proud in the picture. They loved being big brothers to the twins.

One night, Bastian and Dom came into my room to lay with me. I never took the picture out when anyone was around, it was something I did for me. A silent prayer every night for the babies that I missed so much. I don't remember why but that night I decided to share that picture with my boys. Sebastiano just kept staring at that picture while we snuggled together, he fell asleep holding it.

The next day he came to me and asked me if he could have it. I couldn't tell him no, even though it was also the only copy I had at the time. So I wrote on the back of it—the date it was taken and how old they all were. I also wrote a short note to him. I wanted to make sure he knew how much we all loved him. I gave Domenico another picture and wrote to him as well. I always knew it was something they both carried with them, even to this day.

My sweet Bastian,

I hope this picture helps you to always remember the love that you shared with Lorenzo and Giovanna. No matter what happens in your life, they're always with you. Just like Papà, Mam, and Domenico. You're never alone.

Love you forever,

Mam

While I'm standing on the porch, I see the front door slowly open. My beautiful Sebastiano is standing in the doorway. I take two steps and embrace him as tightly as I can. His entire body softens and I feel sobs wracking his body. I try to hold my own back, but his pain is too much for me to handle and my tears flow.

"I'm so sorry, baby. I wish you had told me how much you were hurting. Nothing that has happened is your fault, from the twins being kidnapped to what happened to Schuyler."

I wait for him to calm down, and we go inside. We sit down on the couch. He won't look at me and it's killing me.

"Please look at me, amore."

Sebastiano

I can't bring myself to look at my mam. She's the one person that has never given up on any of us. Even when she wasn't talking to anyone, my three-year-old brain knew she loved us.

Hearing her say nothing was my fault...Dom saw the back of Dorian as he was walking out, but no one knows what I saw.

I saw him carrying Enzo and Gia out of the room.

There was a commotion outside our bedroom door. We all shared a room when we were little. At the time I had no idea what was going on, I didn't know who Dorian was and I thought he'd be back for Dom and me. I thought he had to be a friend of my papà and mam.

He never came back.

Then my parents came in and all I remember is them saying they're gone. Over and over, I watched my mam scream and collapse. She scooped Dom and me up and held us tight as she cried.

CHAPTER TWENTY-ONE

I don't know how to tell my mam that. I could've done something back then.

"Amore, talk to me please. Why did you leave? We all need you just as much as you need us."

I watch the tears roll down my mam's cheeks. I reach out and wipe them off her face.

"I don't know how to be a good papà to my bambino. I couldn't save Enzo and Gia, and Schuyler—she was taken because of me. Conrad was trying to get to me." I choke back a sob.

"I understand that you feel the need to protect all of us. But that isn't something one person can do alone. That's something we do as a family. We take care of each other and when something happens like the kidnappings, it's on all of us. Never one person. When the twins were abducted, that was on your papà and me. Never you and Domenico."

I hear my mam, but my insides are warring with themselves.

"I'm so sorry that I didn't handle their kidnapping better. I wish I could take back that year and spend it holding you and Dom close. Instead I retreated into myself and made you feel like somehow that was your fault. I'll forever be sorry for that." She sobs.

I can't take my mam crying. I slide over to her and hold her tight.

"That wasn't your fault either, Mam. I've always felt that because I was the oldest, it was my responsibility to make sure everyone was okay."

She looks me in the eyes. I can see the hurt in her eyes. But it's not because of me. It's for me.

"I saw Dorian taking them that night," I whisper as I close my eyes.

"Look at me, amore," my mam whispers back to me.

I slowly open my eyes and look at her.

"No matter what you saw that night, you were never to blame for it. You were three years old. Not even old enough to truly remember your baby siblings. And sure as hell not old enough to know that Dorian was taking them from us."

She wraps her arms around me. I can't help the sobs that are wracking my body, but being in my mam's arms soothes me like it did when I was a child.

"I'm so sorry, Mam."

"It's me who's sorry, baby. Please let this part of you go. You're one of the greatest men I know, including your papà and your brothers. I'm so damn proud of who you've become. I could never ask for a better son than you."

"Thank you for never giving up on me, Mam. For always making me feel like I could do anything I wanted to do. And now for helping me to realize that I'm not to blame for Enzo and Gia being taken."

"I wish I'd known that you were carrying that hurt and guilt around with you for so long. I feel like I missed so much with you and Dom. But I will not be missing anything anymore."

I feel like a weight has been lifted as I listen to her. There's always been part of me that knew I couldn't have done anything when the twins were taken. But as their big brother? I just couldn't let that go. And when Schuyler was taken, it brought up all those feelings again.

"Do you think it's time to go back home to Schuyler?"

"Is she angry with me?"

"No, amore, there's no anger from anyone. She's been worried, wanting to help you. And she's scared. Scared that you won't come back to her. Scared that she's done something wrong to make you leave. Just like the rest of us." Mam hugs me as I breathe a sigh of relief. "Sebastiano? Please don't run away again, just talk to us. Every single person in this family would turn the world upside down to help you. Don't you ever forget that."

I look into my mam's blue-green eyes. My eyes.

"I promise, Mam. No more running."

She gives me a small smile.

"But I'm not sure if I'm ready to go home and face Schuyler and everyone yet," I say softly.

I look up at my mam again and she's starting to frown at me.

"Sebastiano Fearghas Mancini! You need to pull your head out of your ass right now. I love you with all that I am, but you need to stop. There's nothing you could've done differently. NOTHING. You've been gone for almost three weeks. It's time to come home and start to heal with all of us. Schuyler and the baby need you. She's been looking forward to her ultrasound appointment tomorrow. But she doesn't want to find out without you."

I know Mam is right. She usually is. But can it really be that simple to go back and have the life I want? I feel my mam's arms wrap around me like a cocoon.

"Let it all out, Bastian. All that anger, fear, and hurt. Let it go," she whispers to me as she rocks me.

I need to go home and make sure Schuyler knows that me leaving had nothing to do with her and everything to do with my own insecurities. She's been my anchor in all of this and yet I've let her down. What kind of man does that? I need to be a better man. Husband. Father. Protector.

Mam's right, it's time to go home.

Chapter Twenty-Two

Schuyler

Another night of going to bed alone. I dream about Sebastiano almost every night. In my dreams, he comes home to me and tells me how much he loves me and that he missed me. I always wake up smiling until I remember that he's not here.

I turn on the TV and get ready for bed. I know he'll come home, I just wish it was now. I stand in front of the bathroom mirror and rub my belly. Since he's been gone, my tummy went from being flat to having a little bump. I can't wait for him to be home so I can show it to him.

Gia, Rella, and I have been texting every night since Bastian left. It's given me so much comfort to have them with me.

Giovanna: How are you and my
niece/nephew doing?

>Schuyler: We're all good. Just getting
ready for bed. How are you guys
doing?

Giovanna: Rowan is being a butt. He
thinks it's fun to keep us up at night. In
fact he's staring at me right now
(Sends a pic of Rowan)

>Schuyler: He's so damn cute. Want me
to come get him so you and Declan
can get a good night's sleep?

Giovanna: I appreciate that, but we're
okay for now. Declan's enjoying it
because he just got home this morning
and he always misses Rowan during
away games

>Fiorella: You two are noisy. Why is no
one talking to me? Rude

I laugh when I see Rella's text. She always keeps us laughing. I don't know what I would do without them. Especially now. They've been my support, keeping me from breaking down.

>Schuyler: Wait. If Declan just got
home, then Cillian just got home too
right? Why aren't you *ahem* making
up for the last week?

Fiorella: OMG. You can just ask why aren't we having sex (scrunched up face emoji) and the answer to that is we did. Now we're done

Giovanna: Wow. Gross. Okay I'm going to go and spend time with my husband and son. Cause EW Rella. Love you both lots

Fiorella: *snicker* Love you, Gia. You going to bed, Skye? We can have hot chocolate if you need company

Schuyler: I'm actually okay tonight, but thank you. I love you both so much

Fiorella: Okay, if you change your mind, I'm right here (purple heart emoji)

Giovanna: We both are (green heart emoji)

Schuyler: (yellow heart emoji)

I love those two so much. I look outside, hoping that wherever Sebastiano is, he's okay. That he can feel how much I love him and need him. How much we love and need him. Staring up at the night sky, I can't help but wonder if he's somewhere looking at the stars too.

Sebastiano

I stare up at the stars. They always make me think of Schuyler.

"I'll be home soon, cuore mio," I say into the night sky.

I head back inside and pack my things, as this will be my last night here. My plan is to get home before Schuyler wakes up. After we had dinner together, I promised Mam that I would go home tonight. She finally left around ten and headed back to her own house, promising she wouldn't tell anyone where I was or that she had talked to me. She's the best woman I know and I'm the man I am because of her and my papà.

Mam told me I need to accept the fact that no matter what, there'll always be things that I can't control. But she understands how hard that is for me to accept. My papà raised Dom and me to be strong and confident but at the same time to have compassion. I grew up watching my papà be a strong man. He has so much love for his family—that was something he never hid from us. He always hugged us and told us how much he loved us.

I just need to learn how to deal with things that I have no control over, because there's going to be a lot of situations like that, especially with having children. And after talking with my mam, I feel more confident that I can do this with Schuyler. We can do this together.

I set my alarm for two in the morning and lay down to nap.

When my alarm goes off, I smile knowing that in a couple of hours I'll have Schuyler back in my arms. And I swear I'll never let her go again. I'm going to make an effort to talk to her more and stop trying to take things on by myself.

I grab my shit and head to the car, making sure to lock the door on the way out. Mam told me to leave the cabin as is and she'll make sure the cleaning crew comes by.

I head to the rental car place and return the SUV, then take a taxi to where I parked my car. I take a deep breath after I get in.

Time to go home.

I can't stop the smile that spreads across my face when I see our house come into view. It's completely dark, so I know everyone's asleep. I don't want to wake any of them. I get out and into the house as quietly as I can.

"Fratello," a voice says from the dark. I jump at least three feet in the fucking air trying not to drop all my shit and wake the rest of the house.

"What the fuck, Dom," I whisper. "Are you trying to give me a heart attack?"

"You should talk. I was up taking a leak and saw headlights pulling into the driveway. You're the fucking creeper, not me."

He pulls me into one of his famous bear hugs.

"I'm so glad you're home, fratello. You've been missed."

I pull back and nod at him. "Thank you for taking care of Schuyler while I was gone."

"Are you okay now?"

"I'm almost there. I promise we'll talk about it, but right now I need my girl."

Another voice comes from the hallway. "You girls are louder than you think. People are trying to sleep."

I chuckle softly.

Nico comes over and gives me a hug. "Good to have you home, Bastian."

"Thanks. And thank you for helping to watch over Schuyler."

"You never have to thank me."

"Okay, before this gets any sappier, go to your girl. She's needed you," Dom says as we all smile.

"I'll see you two in the morning."

I grab my bag and head to our room. I open and close the door as quietly as I can. I put my bag down and stare at my woman. She's even more gorgeous than when I left her. I tiptoe to the bathroom to get undressed. Then I slide into bed with her. She curls herself into me and sighs.

"Cuore mio," I whisper to her.

She turns towards my voice and slowly opens her eyes.

"Am I dreaming?" she asks, putting her hand on my face.

I close my eyes, savoring her touch. "No, amore. You're not. Can you forgive me for leaving?"

She wraps herself around me. "There's no need for forgiveness. But please don't leave me again."

I hear her sniffle and it hurts my heart.

"I promise," I say as I hold her tighter. "I love you so much, Schuyler."

"I love you, Bastian. We love you. Always and unconditionally."

I kiss her, hoping she can feel how much I love her. I truly don't know what I did to deserve her, but I promise myself again that I'll do everything I can to make sure she's happy for the rest of her life.

Chapter Twenty-Three

Schuyler

Waking up is an odd feeling this morning. Part of my brain is remembering Sebastiano coming home early this morning. The other part thinks it was a dream. Then I feel his arm holding me close and I know I wasn't dreaming. He's finally home.

"I can hear you thinking." He chuckles. "Are you ready to find out if we're having a boy or girl? Or do you want to wait and be surprised?"

I turn to face him. "I want both." I giggle as I run my fingers over his tattoos. "What do you want?"

He puts his hand on my belly, "I feel the same way. Why don't we let the bambino choose? If they want to show us they will, if not? We wait."

"That sounds perfect."

I moan softly as he kisses me. It's been three weeks since I felt his lips on me and now I'm certain that I'll never get tired of his kisses. His touch. His fucking magical mouth that's moving down my body.

"Bastian," I moan, grabbing onto his shoulders to pull him back up. "I need to feel you, please."

I reach down and stroke his length.

"Fuck, cuore mio," he gasps. "I need you too."

He pushes into me in one thrust.

"Holy fuck, yes." I bite his chest to keep from screaming his name, grabbing his ass to make him move. He's moving slowly on purpose and it's driving me crazy. "Baby, please."

I hear myself begging him to fuck me. Finally I latch on to the spot on the base of his neck that I know drives him wild. Fuck. Yes.

"Cuore mio," he moans. "Come with me, baby. Please."

His plea hits me and I can't control my body, I can feel him pulsing in me. Which makes my orgasm seem to last forever.

Three weeks is way too long to not have him in my arms and in my body.

Sebastiano

Home.

That's what it is to have Schuyler in my arms again.

Today we get to see the baby. I'm nervous and excited. When we got to hear the baby's heartbeat before, it made me realize I needed to be a better man for my family. I'm still scared as hell to become a papà, but I won't be running away ever again.

Today we'll see if the baby wants to tell us if it's a he or she. And to be honest I don't care either way. I can't wait to meet our baby.

Dom has a game tonight and the whole family is going. I missed three weeks of games while I was gone, but I made sure to watch them on TV. But it doesn't compare to going to live games with everyone.

Sitting and waiting to see the doctor is making me crazy. Who knew waiting could literally make you crazy?

"Are you ok?" I turn and see Schuyler smiling at me. "You look like you're going to throw up."

"I might," I say as I make faces at her. How the fuck is she so calm?

I hold her hand and try to relax. There's a few other couples waiting, like us. I watch as a few get called back. Why isn't it our turn? And why are they staring at me? Is there a booger hanging out of my nose?

We hear someone mention the Redhawks. I get it now, they probably think I'm Dom. I kiss Schuyler's neck.

"They think I'm Dom..." I whisper to her.

She chuckles and nods at me. "Can you blame them? He's known for being single and now they see you here with me."

I put my arm around her and pull her to me. "They could ask instead of staring at me."

"True. But there's a lot of fans who won't come up to someone like Dom. They could be scared or shy."

Schuyler

I can't help but chuckle when I look at Sebastiano. He looks so nervous as we wait for them to call me back. Having him with me makes me feel less anxious.

There are people staring at us, but I'm getting used to that. There are fans who stare at him, thinking he's Domenico.

I can tell them apart. Besides the different tattoos, they walk differently. Dom has a swagger to his walk that my Bastian doesn't have. I think it comes from being in the spotlight so much. Declan, Luca, and Cillian have the same walk.

We finally get called back. I lay back on the exam table while we wait for the doctor.

When my doctor comes in, I see Sebastian's smile turn to a frown.

"I'm Doctor Spencer, you must be dad." He smiles at Bastian.

I can see Dr. Spencer wince slightly as he shakes Sebastiano's hand.

I sigh. That's my baby.

"I see you're here to get your first ultrasound. Did you want to find out the sex?" he asks.

"We do if the baby wants to show us," I answer.

"Okay, let's see if baby will cooperate. This will be a little cold. We try to keep the gel warm, but most people say it's still cold." He chuckles.

I lay back, grabbing Sebastiano's hand and smiling at him.

He squeezes my hand and kisses my forehead. The first thing we hear is baby's heartbeat. It's the most wonderful sound.

"Strong heartbeat. And it looks like baby is moving a lot today."

We watch him move the wand around and it looks like he's snapping screenshots of the baby. The suspense is killing me.

"Congratulations! It's a boy."

"A son," Sebastiano whispers in my ear. "Grazie, cuore mio."

A tear slips out of the corner of my eye when I see the happiness on his face.

"Okay, I'll print out a few of the screenshots and then you can get out of here. You should make your next appointment for four weeks from now. But if you have any questions or feel uncertain about anything, don't hesitate to call or come in."

"Thanks, Doc," Sebastiano says, finally smiling at him.

"You're welcome and congratulations again."

Sebastiano

I've put together the perfect proposal. My whole family is in on it. Surprisingly, no one has spilled the beans to Schuyler, even Rella has somehow managed to stay quiet...

It's nearing the end of the second period and the Redhawks are up 3-0. My time is near. I tell Schuyler that I need the restroom and slip off to get things going.

The buzzer sounds to end the second period. The teams come off the ice and the carpets get rolled out. I can hear the fans around me talking and wondering what is going on.

"Will Miss Schuyler Viñales please come to the hockey helmet concession stand, level two."

She'll know exactly what and where that is. The first game we all went to, the first thing she wanted to do was stop and get a nacho-filled hockey helmet.

I watch from my hiding spot as my two brothers lead her out onto the red carpet. She's so damn beautiful. They stand on both sides of her while I make my way out to her.

When I get to her, I take her hand. She's shaking. The arena is almost completely silent. It's like everyone knows what's about to happen and they're all holding their breath like I am. I drop to one knee.

"Schuyler, my life started the day I met you. That's the day I realized what it felt like to find my soulmate.

The one person that made my life whole. And now you're giving me the greatest gift ever. A family of our own."

Her tears are falling and I'm getting more nervous. But before I can talk myself out of this, I blurt out,

"Marry me. Please."

Schuyler

We watched the red carpet being brought out and like everyone else, I wonder what ceremony is going on tonight.

Hearing my name being called by the announcer, I started to shake. Gia and Rella held each of my hands which helped me to calm down a little. And then I heard where I was supposed to go and I knew who set this up. Is it possible he's going to propose? I've been dreaming about him asking me since the first time he talked about it. I was beginning to think that he changed his mind.

The three of us went to the concession stand and found Domenico and Lorenzo waiting. But no Sebastiano.

They both put their arms out for me to take.

"What's going on?" I ask them. They stare at me and smile. But no one will say anything.

I take both their arms and they lead me to the arena and down to the ice. I can feel every pair of eyes in the arena staring at me and my body is shaking.

Finally I see Sebastiano coming out to join us. He's perfect. And when he drops to one knee in front of me, I can't help the tears. My hand automatically goes to my belly as I listen to him.

"Yes," is all I can choke out.

Sebastiano puts the most beautiful ring on my finger, then picks me up and kisses me. The arena is bursting with everyone cheering for us. Dom and Enzo hug us and follow us off the ice. The rest of the family is waiting for us and we're both engulfed in Mancinis. It's more than I ever imagined my life could be.

Chapter Twenty-Four

Sebastiano

Today I get to marry the other half of my soul. We thought of waiting till after she gives birth, but we both wanted her to have my name now. So we put our wedding together in two short months. I made sure Schuyler got everything she wanted for this day. She's now six months pregnant with our son and just glowing.

Mira is her maid of honor. Gia and Rella are her bridesmaids. Dom is my best man. Enzo, Sal, Luca, Declan, and Cillian are my groomsmen. Yeah, it's a little lopsided, but it works. My papà offered to walk Schuyler down the aisle, but she had already asked Cap, he's more than earned the right to give her away.

As I'm getting ready with all the guys, I finally feel

complete. I'm a very lucky man, I have a twin that has always had my back. Our twin siblings are back with us, and it's like they never left. My parents? I definitely won the lottery there, I don't want to think of what my life would've been like if I had different parents. My uncles, aunt, and cousins, they complete our family in ways I can't even describe. And today? Today my circle will be complete when Schuyler Elena Viñales becomes Schuyler Elena Mancini.

Schuyler

Today is really here. The day that I dreamed of as a little girl. I get to marry my Prince Charming.

I look at my belly in the mirror, the dress I'm wearing hugs me in all the right places without making me look like a beached whale.

Mama Lynn, Mam Gráinne, Rosaura, Mirabelle, Giovanna, and Fiorella are in the room with me. Six of the best women I know, strong, beautiful and best of all? They're my family. My children will grow up with the strong men of the Mancini family and with them, the strong women that keep this family together.

"I'm so happy that you've found your prince." Mira smiles at me. "And thank you for being okay with me and Nico."

I hug her tight. "I know Nico will treat you right. I'm so happy that you've found each other."

"Just know that if by any chance Nico does hurt you? There's a whole line of alpha Mancini men waiting to take care of him." Gia snickers.

Mam Gráinne laughs. "That's the truth, the Mancini men are not going to let anyone hurt our Mira."

My smile gets bigger as I watch my baby sister blush at their words. She always told me she wanted a big brother, and now she has five of them.

"Today is everything I've wanted for you, Schuyler. The day that Michael brought you both home to me, I knew you were both so special. You're the daughters that I dreamed about." Mama sniffles as she hugs Mira and me tight.

"I'll be forever grateful that we found you and Cap. I could never have made it through those first years of trying to work and raise Mira at the same time without you. Thank you for being the parents that I wished for."

All eight of us come together in a hug. These women are so fucking incredible. I'm trying not to burst into tears and ruin the makeup they spent so much time on. But between these damn hormones and all this love, I lose the battle.

After I get my crying under control, they all help me get my face cleaned up.

There's a knock at the door. Mam Gráinne goes over and cracks it open.

"Colomba mia, are you all ready? It's time," Enea's accented voice floats into the room.

"Sì, amore mio, we're ready." She opens the door to reveal Enea, Leonardo, Antonio, Domenico, Declan, Cillian, and Cap. Such a handsome bunch.

My heart is bursting as I watch each of them take their woman and head into the church. Domenico takes Mira's hand to lead her to their places.

Antonio takes Mama Lynn's hand and as she walks by Cap, she gives him a kiss.

"Take care of our girl," she whispers to him.

"Always," he responds.

I take one last look at myself in the mirror. The next time I do this, I'll be Schuyler Mancini.

"You ready, baby?" Cap looks at me with tears in his eyes.

"I'm ready, Dad," I say softly.

He grabs me, holding me tight as he sniffles. "I'm so sorry I didn't see what Blaine was doing to you. And I'm so glad you found Sebastiano, he's a great man and the only one I would give you away to."

"You did everything right. You've been the father I never had but always wanted. You and Mama gave us a home and a family."

His tears are falling while he listens to me, and he hugs me again. "Those damn Mancinis have me wanting to give out more hugs. Dammit."

I chuckle. "Yeah, they really do love hugging."

"Okay, sweet girl, let's get you married."

Sebastiano

Watching everyone walk into the church to their places, is making me anxious. I need to see my girl—she wanted to be traditional, so I haven't seen her for two days.

When the music starts, my heart starts racing as the doors open to reveal the most beautiful woman I've ever seen. Schuyler looks like an angel floating towards me. I take a step forward and wait.

"Who gives this woman to this man?" Father Bianco asks.

"Her mother and I do." Cap's voice is clear.

Father Bianco nods and steps back so that Cap can put Schuyler's hand in mine.

"I know you'll take good care of her, son. I'm proud to welcome you into our family as you've welcomed us into yours."

"I'll always take care of her. I promise you that."

We both watch Cap go over and sit with Lynn.

Then we turn to each other and Father Bianco starts.

"Sebastiano and Schuyler have written their own vows."

"Cuore mio. I never believed in soulmates, but the moment I saw you, I knew they were real. There's one perfect person for each of us and I'm lucky to have you as mine. I promise to always love you and our children. Thank you for making me the happiest man alive."

Schuyler's eyes are shining with her unshed tears. She clears her throat and starts her vows.

"Sebastiano, before we met, I thought I was doomed to a life of sadness. Then I met you and it was like a veil was lifted off of my eyes. For the first time in a long time, I saw a future I actually wanted to be a part of. You did that. You gave me hope and today you made another dream of mine come true. I get to marry my best friend, my prince."

I lean over and kiss her softly.

Father Bianco clears his throat. "We haven't gotten to that part yet, Sebastiano."

Everyone in the church laughs.

"Mi dispiace, Padre." I smile.

He smiles back at us.

"Sebastiano Fearghas Mancini and Schuyler Elena Viñales, have you come here freely and without reservation to give yourselves to each other in marriage?"

We both respond yes.

"Will you honor each other as man and wife for the rest of your lives?"

Again we say yes.

"Will you accept children lovingly from God, and raise them according to the law of Christ and his church?"

For a third time, we say yes.

"Sebastiano, please repeat after me. I, Sebastiano Fearghas Mancini, take you, Schuyler Elena Viñales, to be my wife. I promise to be true to you in good times and in bad, in sickness and in health. I will love you and honor you all the days of my life."

I look into Schuyler's beautiful blue eyes and repeat after Father Bianco.

"Schuyler, please repeat after me. I, Schuyler Elena Viñales, take you, Sebastiano Fearghas Mancini, to be my husband. I promise to be true to you in good times and in bad, in sickness and in health. I will love you and honor you all the days of my life."

Schuyler repeats after Father Bianco, and he smiles. "I have the great honor of introducing you all to Mr. and Mrs. Sebastiano and Schuyler Mancini. Now you can kiss your bride." He winks at me and chuckles.

I wrap my arms around Schuyler and kiss her with all the passion I can show her. My wife.

Epilogue

Schuyler

Our son decided to make his appearance on his cousin Rowan's first birthday. I love that this is something they'll share for the rest of their lives. We named him Sansone Emiliano Mancini. Sansone is the Italian version of Samson so we call him Sam or Sammy. He has his papà's blue-green eyes and my dark hair.

I've been through so much these last few years. Hell, if I think about it, it's been a pattern throughout my whole life. But meeting Sebastiano has changed that. He helped me break the cycle and find a new way to live. One that makes what I want a priority and not an inconvenience.

It's been two months since Sansone was born and tonight we're having a celebration to make up for disrupting Rowan's first birthday party. Everyone is here, including Elio, his crew, and the Cimaruta MC. I can't wait until Sammy is old enough to play with Rowan and Grayson.

Cap comes over and takes Sam from me.

"Come hang out with your grandpa and nonno." He smiles, taking Sam over to Enea.

I see Enea smiling at Sammy. It warms my heart to see how loved my son is. I know that no matter what happens, he will always have the support of this entire family.

"Hey Skye," Gia says as she sits down next to me. "How are things with my brother? Have you two talked about why he left?"

"We have, there's more we need to talk about, but everything has been really good. I understand now why Bastian felt that he had to leave, it still hurts but I do get it. And I'm happy that he's found some peace with the past."

Gia nods. "I understand completely. When I found Declan, I was going through a lot. Enzo and I had just learned about being kidnapped. I felt like my whole world was crashing down on me. But he never gave up on me and helped me to see that I can get through anything with him by my side. You and Bastian have that too. I know he needed to get his head on straight, but now he's on the right path." She takes a deep breath. "You should've seen the things I put Declan through. When I think about it now, I'm amazed that he didn't leave me."

I smile at Gia. This isn't the first time she's talked to me about what went on with her and Declan. But each time we talk, she tells me a little more about what she went through. It also makes me feel closer to her knowing she has that kind of faith in Bastian and me.

"I'm really glad that Bastian has you. When you and I first met, I was worried about him. I still worry about Dom. They carried so much guilt over what happened to us that they never let anyone in. Now that Bastian has you, maybe Dom will finally find his forever too."

"I think in time he will, it's when you least expect it. That's when your person comes to you. I never thought I could get away from Blaine. But look at me now, your brother has made all of my dreams come true."

I know this is my forever. There is no one I could ever want more than Sebastiano. No matter what lifetime we're in.

Sebastiano

Things have changed so much in the last two years. Losing Enzo and Gia—that was just the start of the crazy rollercoaster of my life.

When we found them, I thought nothing could top that. Then I met Schuyler. And I realized how wrong I was. She has brought so much to my life and I can hardly remember what it was like before her. And now we're married and have a son. I'm a papà. I still can't believe it.

I watch my papà and Cap with my son. The looks on their faces are of pure joy.

Salvatore comes over to me. "You look happy, cugino."

"I am happy. Thank you for everything you've done for Schuyler and for me. I don't even want to think about how it could've turned out if we didn't have your help."

"Familigia, cugino. There's never anything I wouldn't do for any of you."

My cousin could've lost his job because of the situation with Blaine and Conrad. But that never made a difference to him, he never stopped fighting for us. Thanks to everyone's help, my wife and son are safe. I'm forever grateful to all of them.

"How are things with you and Schuyler?"

"Things are going good. I'm still so grateful that she wasn't angry with me for leaving. I was worried that she wouldn't understand why I had to do it. I'm a lucky man."

"You are, cugino. I can only hope that one day I'll be just as lucky.'

"You will. After meeting Schuyler, I believe there's someone for all of us. It's just timing."

Salvatore gives me a small smile. "I can dream, cugino."

About the Author

Hi! I'm Natalie. I published my first book, Aftermath in August 2021. I've been lucky enough to find my own insta-love-at-first-sight person. We have a daughter who drives us crazy and a corgi who adds to the chaos. I love hockey (Chicago Blackhawks), MotoGP (Motorcycle Racing), and baseball (Chicago Cubs). When I'm not writing, you can find me studying or crafting. Or crafting when I should be studying.

Nataliearthurbooks.com

Giovanna

Everything I thought about my life was a lie and because of that, trust became non-existent for me. Then I met Declan. He pushed his way into my life, determined to prove to me that not everyone is a liar. He's a hockey player and we all know the reputation of hockey players. But I want to trust someone again…maybe he's the one?

<u>Declan</u>

Hockey has been my focus for as long as I can remember. The day I met Giovanna, my life changed. Hockey would always be my first love. But she would be my last. Something happened to her and she's afraid to trust me. But that's okay, I'll show her that I'm real. That we're real.

Aftermath is the first book in my Mancini Legacy Series. All books are standalone, but it's best if read in order. There is mention of characters from my Cimaruta MC Chicago Series.

https://books2read.com/Aftermath-ManciniLegacy

Luciana

Women on an MC council? It's unheard of until now. Love at first sight? That's a new one for me too. I was convinced I didn't need someone to make me happy.

Then I slammed into Rónán.

Literally.

In an instant, he turned my world upside down. But can he handle the MC life?

<u>**Rónán**</u>

My life was going the way I planned it. Then the most beautiful woman stepped into my path and changed my life forever. I know she's keeping things from me. And that's okay...for now.

Because she's mine.

She just doesn't know it yet.

Choices is the first book in my Cimaruta MC Chicago Series. All books are standalone, but it's best if read in order. There is mention of characters from my Mancini Legacy Series.

https://books2read.com/Choices-CimarutaMCChicago

Francesco

I met the love of my life at fourteen. She had my heart the moment I saw her. But when you're young and stupid you don't always make the right decisions. That's what happened to me. I let the temptations of my job distract me from the one thing I couldn't live without. I had lost all hope, but fate gave me another chance. I have to make it up to her. I know she's hiding something from me. Will she let me in and give me a second chance?

<u>**Maeve**</u>

I thought I had it all. Sure I may have been young, but when it's real, you just know. That was, until he ended things. I never saw it coming. Now he's back and he wants another chance. Can I really trust him not to break my heart again? I want to believe him. I've never stopped loving him. But it's not just me I have to protect anymore.

Can they find their way back to the happily ever after they were meant to have? Or will they be pulled apart again, shattering all hope?

Reclaiming Our Forever is the second book in my Cimaruta MC Chicago Series. All books are standalone, but it's best if read in order. There is mention of characters from my Mancini Legacy Series.

https://books2read.com/ReclaimingOurForever-CimarutaMCChicago

Amante

Relationship? No.

Love? Hell no.

Forever? Never.

A quick hook up and that was that. I had my family and my club and that's all I needed. Until the day she walked in. With her I wanted more than one night, but when I got out of the shower she was gone. But I will find her. Then I'll just have to convince her we belong together.

<u>Charmaine</u>

Love is nothing but a lie. I watched my parents crash and burn and nothing and no one could change my mind. Until him. My tattooed, hunky biker man. Wait, did I say mine? That can't happen. But he says all the right things, and makes me feel like I'm the most special girl in the world. Can we make it work?

Notch the Plan is part of the Notchin' Boots Series. There is mention of characters from my Mancini Legacy Series and my Cimaruta MC Chicago Series.

https://books2read.com/NotchThePlan-NotchinBoots

<u>Hollis</u>

The people you're born to don't always turn out to be your 'family'. Families can be chosen, and I chose the Cimaruta MC. They've been there with me for the last six years, and I thought I had everything I needed. One night was all it took to make me want more. But she's hiding something from me and I need to know what it is. I will save her from anything. That much I do know.

<u>Lila</u>

My life was finally going smoothly. It was me and my daughter against the world. I worked at a club called Club Curve—I'm a curvy girl, so why not? Then one night, HE walked in. Now he's turning my life upside down and I'm not sure how to feel about it. My biggest fear is about to become a reality.

Just as you are is a stand alone and part of the Club Curve series. But there is mention of characters from my Mancini Legacy and Cimaruta MC Chicago series.

https://books2read.com/JustAsYouAre-ClubCurve

Kostas

Mating matches keep the peace in our world. So why did it feel like my life was over when it was my turn? She hated me from the moment we were paired. And to be honest? I hated her too. So when she rejected me for some loser from another clan, it didn't bother me that much. But then I met her—the one the fates chose for me—and everything just felt right. I knew in an instant that she was the one I would never let go of.

Artemis

In our world, mates can be either fated or chosen, but finding your fated mate is never guaranteed. I thought I had chosen someone who could love me and we would spend our lives together. But then he rejected me—for my BEST FRIEND. That day, I decided I was fine being alone. But then, completely by chance, I met someone who felt like home. Could this really be it? The forever I secretly craved...my fated one.

My Fated One is part of the Fated Mates Series. There is mention of characters from my Mancini Legacy Series and my Cimaruta MC Chicago Series.

https://books2read.com/MyFatedOne-FatedMates

Aiden

Motorcycle racing has been my life since I could walk and talk. It was all I ever needed. Or so I thought. Then I met the one woman that made me want more. One day, the unthinkable happens—a racing accident causes me to lose all my memories of her. But I still feel her in my soul, even if my brain can't remember her.

Élodie

I wanted a knight in shining armor, but what I got was a wolf in disguise. After escaping from him, I met a man willing to give me everything I ever wanted. Then in a split second, he was taken from me. Not physically, but mentally. The man I love doesn't remember who I am, but I'm determined to get him back.

Racing Back to Love is part of the Forget-Me-Not Series. There is mention of characters from my Mancini Legacy Series.

https://books2read.com/RacingBackToLove-ForgetMeNot